Mary De Morgan, und Andere

The Necklace of Princess Fiorimonde

And other Stories

Mary De Morgan, und Andere

The Necklace of Princess Fiorimonde
And other Stories

ISBN/EAN: 9783744750110

Printed in Europe, USA, Canada, Australia, Japan

Cover: Foto ©Andreas Hilbeck / pixelio.de

More available books at **www.hansebooks.com**

THE NECKLACE
OF
PRINCESS FIORIMONDE;
AND OTHER STORIES
BY
MARY DE MORGAN
[Author of "On a Pincushion"]

WITH

ILLUSTRATIONS

BY

WALTER

CRANE

LONDON:

MACMILLAN & CO:
1886.

CONTENTS.

LIST OF ILLUSTRATIONS.

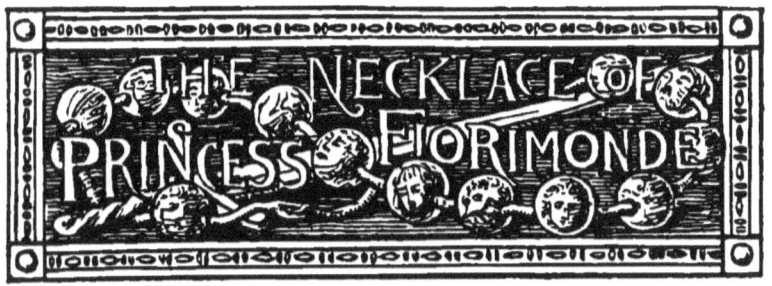

 NCE there lived a King, whose wife was dead, but who had a most beautiful daughter— so beautiful that every one thought she must be good as well, instead of which the Princess was really very wicked, and practised witchcraft and black magic, which she had learned from an old witch who lived in a hut on the side of a lonely mountain. This old witch was wicked and hideous, and no one but the King's daughter knew that she lived there; but at night, when every one else was asleep, the Princess, whose name was Fiorimonde, used to visit her by stealth to learn sorcery.

It was only the witch's arts which had made Fiorimonde so beautiful that there was no one like her in the world, and in return the Princess helped her with all her tricks, and never told any one she was there.

The time came when the King began to think he should like his daughter to marry, so he summoned his council and said, "We have no son to reign after our death, so we had best seek for a suitable prince to marry to our royal daughter, and then, when we are too old, he shall be king in our stead." And all the council said he was very wise, and it would be well for the Princess to marry. So heralds were sent to all the neighbouring kings and princes to say that the King would choose a husband for the Princess, who should be king after him. But when Fiorimonde heard this she wept with rage, for she knew quite well that if she had a husband he would find out how she went to visit the old witch, and would stop her practising magic, and then she would lose her beauty.

When night came, and every one in the

palace was fast asleep, the Princess went to her
bedroom window and softly opened it. Then
she took from her pocket a handful of peas and
held them out of the window and chirruped low,
and there flew down from the roof a small
brown bird and sat upon her wrist and began
to eat the peas. No sooner had it swallowed
them than it began to grow and grow and grow
till it was so big that the Princess could not
hold it, but let it stand on the window-sill, and
still it grew and grew and grew till it was as
large as an ostrich. Then the Princess climbed
out of the window and seated herself on the
bird's back, and at once it flew straight away
over the tops of the trees till it came to the
mountain where the old witch dwelt, and
stopped in front of the door of her hut.

The Princess jumped off, and muttered
some words through the keyhole, when a
croaking voice from within called,

"Why do you come to-night? Have I not
told you I wished to be left alone for thirteen
nights; why do you disturb me?"

"But I beg of you to let me in," said the

Princess, "for I am in trouble and want your help."

"Come in then," said the voice; and the door flew open, and the Princess trod into the hut, in the middle of which, wrapped in a gray cloak which almost hid her, sat the witch. Princess Fiorimonde sat down near her, and told her, her story. How the King wished her to marry, and had sent word to the neighbouring princes, that they might make offers for her.

"This is truly bad hearing," croaked the witch, "but we shall beat them yet; and you must deal with each Prince as he comes. Would you like them to become dogs, to come at your call, or birds, to fly in the air, and sing of your beauty, or will you make them all into beads, the beads of such a necklace as never woman wore before, so that they may rest upon your neck, and you may take them with you always."

"The necklace! the necklace!" cried the Princess, clapping her hands with joy. "That will be best of all, to sling them upon a string and wear them around my throat. Little will the courtiers know whence come my new jewels."

"But this is a dangerous play," quoth the witch, "for, unless you are very careful, you yourself may become a bead and hang upon the string with the others, and there you will remain till some one cuts the string, and draws you off."

"Nay, never fear," said the Princess, "I will be careful, only tell me what to do, and I will have great princes and kings to adorn me, and all their greatness shall not help them."

Then the witch dipped her hand into a black bag which stood on the ground beside her, and drew out a long gold thread.

The ends were joined together, but no one could see the joins, and however much you pulled, it would not break. It would easily go over Fiorimonde's head, and the witch slipped it on her neck saying,

"Now mind, while this hangs here you are safe enough, but if once you join your fingers around the string you too will meet the fate of

your lovers, and hang upon it yourself. As for·
the kings and princes who would marry you, all
you have to do is to make them close their
fingers around the chain, and at once they
will be strung upon it as bright hard beads,
and there they shall remain, till it is cut and
they drop off."

"This is really delightful," cried the Princess; "and I am already quite impatient for
the first to come that I may try."

"And now," said the witch, "since you
are here, and there is yet time, we will have a
dance, and I will summon the guests." So
saying, she took from a corner a drum and a
pair of drum-sticks, and going to the door,
began to beat upon it. It made a terrible
rattling. In a moment came flying through
the air all sorts of forms. There were little
dark elves with long tails, and goblins who
chattered and laughed, and other witches who
rode on broom-sticks. There was one wicked
fairy in the form of a large cat, with bright
green eyes, and another came sliding in like a
long shining viper.

Then, when all had arrived, the witch
stopped drumming, and, going to the middle of
the hut, stamped on the floor, and a trap-door
opened in the ground. The old witch stepped
through it, and led the way down a narrow dark
passage, to a large underground chamber, and
all her strange guests followed, and here they
all danced and made merry in a terrible way,
but at first sound of cock-crow all the guests
disappeared with a whiff, and the Princess
hastened up the dark passage again, and out of
the hut to where her big bird still waited for
her, and mounting its back she flew home in a
trice. Then, when she had stepped in at her
bedroom window, she poured into a cup from
a small black bottle, a few drops of magic water,
and gave it to the bird to drink, and as it sipped
it grew smaller, and smaller, till at last it had
quite regained its natural size, and hopped on to
the roof as before, and the Princess shut her
window, and got into bed, and fell asleep, and
no one knew of her strange journey, or where
she had been.

Next day Fiorimonde declared to her father

the King, that she was quite willing to wed any prince he should fix upon as a husband for her, at which he was much pleased, and soon after informed her, that a young king was coming from over the sea to be her husband. He was king of a large rich country, and would take back his bride with him to his home. He was called King Pierrot. Great preparations were made for his arrival, and the Princess was decked in her finest array to greet him, and when he came all the courtiers said, "This is truly a proper husband for our beautiful Princess," for he was strong and handsome, with black hair, and eyes like sloes. King Pierrot was delighted with Fiorimonde's beauty, and was happy as the day is long; and all things went merrily till the evening before the marriage. A great feast was held, at which the Princess looked lovelier than ever dressed in a red gown, the colour of the inside of a rose, but she wore no jewels nor ornaments of any kind, save one shining gold string round her milk-white throat.

When the feast was done, the Princess stepped from her golden chair at her father's side, and walked softly into the garden, and stood under an elm-tree looking at the shining moon. In a few moments King Pierrot followed her, and stood beside her, looking at her and wondering at her beauty.

"To-morrow, then, my sweet Princess, you will be my Queen, and share all I possess. What gift would you wish me to give you on our wedding day?"

"I would have a necklace wrought of the finest gold and jewels to be found, and just the length of this gold cord which I wear around my throat," answered Princess Fiorimonde.

"Why do you wear that cord?" asked King Pierrot; "it has no jewel nor ornament about it."

"Nay, but there is no cord like mine in all the world," cried Fiorimonde, and her eyes sparkled wickedly as she spoke; "it is as light as a feather, but stronger than an iron chain. Take it in both hands and try to break it, that you may see how strong it is;" and King Pierrot took the cord in both hands to pull it hard; but no sooner were his fingers closed around it than he vanished like a puff of smoke, and on the cord appeared a bright, beautiful bead—so bright and beautiful as was never bead before—clear as crystal, but shining with all colours—green, blue, and gold.

Princess Fiorimonde gazed down at it and laughed aloud.

"Aha, my proud lover! are you there?" she cried with glee; "my necklace bids fair to beat all others in the world," and she caressed the bead with the tips of her soft, white fingers, but was careful that they did not close round the string. Then she returned into the banqueting hall, and spoke to the King.

"Pray, sire," said she, "send some one at once to find King Pierrot, for, as he was talking to me a minute ago, he suddenly left me, and I am afraid lest I may have given him offence, or perhaps he is ill.

The King desired that the servants should seek for King Pierrot all over the grounds, and seek him they did, but nowhere was he to be found, and the old King looked offended.

"Doubtless he will be ready to-morrow in time for the wedding," quoth he, "but we are not best pleased that he should treat us in this way."

Princess Fiorimonde had a little maid called Yolande. She was a bright-faced girl with merry brown eyes, but she was not beautiful like Fiorimonde, and she did not love her mistress, for she was afraid of her, and suspected her of her wicked ways. When she undressed her that night she noticed the gold cord, and the one bright bead upon it, and as she combed the Princess's hair she looked over her shoulder into the looking-glass, and saw how she laughed, and how fondly she looked at the cord, and caressed the bead, again and again with her fingers.

" That is a wonderful bead on your Highness's cord," said Yolande, looking at its reflection in the mirror ; "surely it must be a bridal gift from King Pierrot."

"And so it is, little Yolande," cried Fiorimonde, laughing merrily ; "and the best gift he could give me. But I think one bead alone looks ugly and ungainly ; soon I hope I shall have another, and another, and another, all as beautiful as the first."

Then Yolande shook her head, and said to herself, "This bodes no good."

Next morning all was prepared for the marriage, and the Princess was dressed in white satin and pearls with a long white lace veil over her, and a bridal wreath on her head, and she stood waiting among her grandly dressed ladies, who all said that such a beautiful bride had never been seen in the world before. But just as they were preparing to go down to the fine company in the hall, a messenger came in great haste summoning the Princess at once to her father the King, as he was much perplexed.

"My daughter," cried he, as Fiorimonde in all her bridal array entered the room where he sat alone, "what can we do? King Pierrot is nowhere to be found; I fear lest he may have been seized by robbers and basely murdered for his rich clothes, or carried away to some mountain and left there to starve. My soldiers are gone far and wide to seek him—and we shall hear of him ere day is done—but where there is no bridegroom there can be no bridal."

"Then let it be put off, my father," cried the Princess, "and to-morrow we shall know if it is for a wedding, or a funeral, we must dress ;" and she pretended to weep, but even then could hardly keep from laughing.

So the wedding guests went away, and the Princess laid aside her bridal dress, and all waited anxiously for news of King Pierrot; and no news came. So at last every one gave him up for dead, and mourned for him, and wondered how he had met his fate.

Princess Fiorimonde put on a black gown, and begged to be allowed to live in seclusion for one month in which to grieve for King Pierrot; but when she was again alone in her bedroom she sat before her looking-glass and laughed till tears ran down her cheeks; and Yolande watched her, and trembled, when she heard her laughter She noticed, too, that beneath her black gown, the Princess still wore her gold cord, and did not move it night or day.

The month had barely passed away when

the King came to his daughter, and announced that another suitor had presented himself, whom he should much like to be her husband. The Princess agreed quite obediently to all her father said; and it was arranged that the marriage should take place. This new prince was called Prince Hildebrandt. He came from a country far north, of which one day he would be king. He was tall, and fair, and strong, with flaxen hair and bright blue eyes. When Princess Fiorimonde saw his portrait she was much pleased, and said, " By all means let him come, and the sooner the better." So she put off her black clothes, and again great preparations were made for a wedding; and King Pierrot was quite forgotten.

Prince Hildebrandt came, and with him many fine gentlemen, and they brought beautiful gifts for the bride. The evening of his arrival all went well, and again there was a grand feast, and Fiorimonde looked so beautiful that Prince Hildebrandt was delighted; and this time she did not leave her father's side, but sat by him all the evening.

Early next morning at sunrise, when every
one was still sleeping, the Princess rose, and
dressed herself in a plain white gown, and
brushed all her hair over her shoulders, and
crept quietly downstairs into the palace gardens;
then she walked on till she came beneath the
window of Prince Hildebrandt's room, and here
she paused and began to sing a little song as
sweet and joyous as a lark's. When Prince
Hildebrandt heard it he got up and went to the
window and looked out to see who sang, and
when he saw Fiorimonde standing in the red
sunrise-light, which made her hair look gold, and
her face rosy, he made haste to dress himself
and go down to meet her.

" How, my Princess," cried he, as he stepped
into the garden beside her. " This is indeed
great happiness to meet you here so early. Tell
me why do you come out at sunrise to sing by
yourself ?"

" I come that I may see the colours of
the sky—red, blue, and gold," answered the
Princess. " Look, there are no such colours
to be seen anywhere, unless, indeed, it be

in this bead which I wear here on my golden cord.

"What is that bead, and where did it come from?" asked Hildebrandt.

"It came from over the sea, where it shall never return again," answered the Princess. And again her eyes began to sparkle with eagerness, and she could scarcely conceal her mirth. "Lift the cord off my neck and look at it near, and tell me if you ever saw one like it."

Hildebrandt put out his hands and took hold of the cord, but no sooner were his fingers closed around it than he vanished, and a new bright bead was slung next to the first one on Fiorimonde's chain, and this one was even more beautiful than the other.

The Princess gave a long low laugh, quite terrible to hear.

"Oh, my sweet necklace," cried she, "how beautiful you are growing! I think I love you more than anything in the world besides." Then she went softly back to bed, without any one hearing her, and fell sound asleep, and slept till Yolande came to tell her it was time for her to get up and dress for the wedding.

The Princess was dressed in gorgeous clothes, and only Yolande noticed that beneath her satin gown, she wore the golden cord, but now there were two beads upon it instead of one. Scarcely was she ready when the King burst into her room in a towering rage.

"My daughter," cried he, "there is a plot against us. Lay aside your bridal attire and think no more of Prince Hildebrandt, for he too has disappeared, and is nowhere to be found."

At this the Princess wept, and entreated that Hildebrandt should be sought for far and near, but she laughed to herself, and said, "Search where you will, yet you shall not find him;" and so again a great search was made, and when no trace of the Prince was found, all the palace was in an uproar.

The Princess again put off her bride's dress and clad herself in black, and sat alone, and pretended to weep, but Yolande, who watched her, shook her head, and said, "More will come

c

and go before the wicked Princess has done her worst."

A month passed, in which Fiorimonde pretended to mourn for Hildebrandt, then she went to the King and said,

"Sire, I pray that you will not let people say that when any bridegroom comes to marry me, as soon as he has seen me he flies rather than be my husband. I beg that suitors may be summoned from far and near that I may not be left alone unwed."

The King agreed, and envoys were sent all the world over to bid any who would come and be the husband of Princess Fiorimonde. And come they did, kings and princes from south and north, east and west,—King Adrian, Prince Sigbert, Prince Algar, and many more,—but though all went well till the wedding morning, when it was time to go to church, no bridegroom was to be found. The old King was sadly frightened, and would fain have given up all hope of finding a husband for the Princess, but now she implored him, with tears in her eyes, not to let her be disgraced in this way.

And so suitor after suitor continued to come, and now it was known, far and wide, that whoever came to ask for the hand of Princess Fiori-monde vanished, and was seen no more of men. The courtiers were afraid and whispered under their breath, " It is not all right, it cannot be ;" but only Yolande noticed how the beads came upon the golden thread, till it was well-nigh covered, yet there always was room for one bead more.

So the years passed, and every year Princess Fiorimonde grew lovelier and lovelier, so that no one who saw her could guess how wicked she was.

In a far off country lived a young prince whose name was Florestan. He had a dear friend named Gervaise, whom he loved better than any one in the world. Gervaise was tall, and broad, and stout of limb, and he loved Prince Florestan so well, that he would gladly have died to serve him.

It chanced that Prince Florestan saw a portrait of Princess Fiorimonde, and at once swore he would go to her father's court, and beg that he might have her for his wife, and Gervaise in vain tried to dissuade him.

"There is an evil fate about the Princess Fiorimonde," quoth he; "many have gone to marry her, but where are they now?"

"I don't know or care," answered Florestan, "but this is sure, that I will wed her and return here, and bring my bride with me."

So he set out for Fiorimonde's home, and Gervaise went with him with a heavy heart.

When they reached the court, the old King received them and welcomed them warmly, and he said to his courtiers, "Here is a fine young prince to whom we would gladly see our daughter wed. Let us hope that this time all will be well." But now Fiorimonde had grown so bold, that she scarcely tried to conceal her mirth.

"I will gladly marry him to-morrow, if he comes to the church," she said; "but if he is not there, what can I do," and she laughed long and merrily, till those who heard her shuddered.

When the Princess's ladies came to tell her

that Prince Florestan was arrived, she was in the garden, lying on the marble edge of a fountain, feeding the gold fish who swam in the water.

" Bid him come to me," she said, "for I will not go any more in state to meet any suitors, neither will I put on grand attire for them. Let him come and find me as I am, since all find it so easy to come and go." So her ladies told the prince that Fiorimonde waited for him near the fountain.

She did not rise when he came to where she lay, but his heart bounded with joy, for he had never in his life beheld such a beautiful woman.

She wore a thin soft white dress, which clung to her lithe figure. Her beautiful arms and hands were bare, and she dabbled with them in the water, and played with the fish. Her great blue eyes were sparkling with mirth, and were so beautiful, that no one noticed the wicked look hid in them; and on her neck lay the marvellous many-coloured necklace, which was itself a wonder to behold.

" You have my best greetings, Prince Florestan," she said. "And you, too, would be my
suitor. Have you thought well of what you
would do, since so many princes who have seen
me have fled for ever, rather than marry me ?"
and as she spoke, she raised her white hand
from the water, and held it out to the Prince,
who stooped and kissed it, and scarcely knew
how to answer her for bewilderment at her
great loveliness.

Gervaise followed his master at a short
distance, but he was ill at ease, and trembled
for fear of what should come.

"Come, bid your friend leave us," said
Fiorimonde, looking at Gervaise, "and sit beside me, and tell me of your home, and why
you wish to marry me, and all pleasant things."

Florestan begged that Gervaise would leave
them for a little, and he walked slowly away,
in a very mournful mood.

He went on down the walks, not heeding
where he was going, till he met Yolande, who
stood beneath a tree laden with rosy apples,
picking the fruit, and throwing it into a basket

at her feet. He would have passed her in silence, but she stopped him, and said,

"Have you come with the new Prince? Do you love your master?"

"Ay, better than any one else on the earth," answered Gervaise. "Why do you ask?"

"And where is he now," said Yolande, not heeding Gervaise's question.

"He sits by the fountain with the beautiful Princess," said Gervaise.

"Then, I hope you have said good-bye to him well, for be assured you shall never see him again," said Yolande nodding her head.

"Why not, and who are you to talk like this?" asked Gervaise.

"My name is Yolande," answered she, "and I am Princess Fiorimonde's maid. Do you not know that Prince Florestan is the eleventh lover who has come to marry her, and one by one they have disappeared, and only I know where they are gone."

"And where are they gone?" cried Gervaise, "and why do you not tell the world, and prevent good men being lost like this?"

" Because I fear my mistress," said Yolande, speaking low and drawing near to him; "she is a sorceress, and she wears the brave kings and princes who come to woo her, strung upon a cord round her neck. Each one forms the bead of a necklace which she wears, both day and night. I have watched that necklace growing; first it was only an empty gold thread; then came King Pierrot, and when he disappeared the first bead appeared upon it. Then came Hildebrandt, and two beads were on the string instead of one; then followed Adrian, Sigbert, and Algar, and Cenred, and Pharamond, and Baldwyn, and Leofric, and Raoul, and all are gone, and ten beads hang upon the string, and to-night there will be eleven, and the eleventh will be your Prince Florestan."

" If this be so," cried Gervaise, " I will never rest till I have plunged my sword into Fiorimonde's heart;" but Yolande shook her head.

" She is a sorceress," she said, "and it might be hard to kill her; besides, that might not break the spell, and bring back the princes to

life. I wish I could show you the necklace,
and you might count the beads, and see if I do
not speak truth, but it is always about her neck,
both night and day, so it is impossible."

"Take me to her room to-night when
she is asleep, and let me see it there," said
Gervaise.

"Very well, we will try," said Yolande; "but
you must be very still, and make no noise, for
if she wakes, remember it will be worse for us
both."

When night came and all in the palace were
fast asleep, Gervaise and Yolande met in the
great hall, and Yolande told him that the
Princess slumbered soundly.

"So now let us go," said she, "and I will
show you the necklace on which Fiorimonde
wears her lovers strung like beads, though how
she transforms them I know not."

"Stay one instant, Yolande," said Gervaise,
holding her back, as she would have tripped
upstairs. "Perhaps, try how I may, I shall be
beaten, and either die or become a bead like
those who have come before me. But if I

succeed and rid the land of your wicked Princess, what will you promise me for a reward?"

"What would you have?" asked Yolande.

"I would have you say you will be my wife, and come back with me to my own land," said Gervaise.

"That I will promise gladly," said Yolande, kissing him, "but we must not speak or think of this till we have cut the cord from Fiorimonde's neck, and all her lovers are set free."

So they went softly up to the Princess's room, Yolande holding a small lantern, which gave only a dim light. There, in her grand bed, lay Princess Fiorimonde. They could just see her by the lantern's light, and she looked so beautiful that Gervaise began to think Yolande spoke falsely, when she said she was so wicked.

Her face was calm and sweet as a baby's; her hair fell in ruddy waves on the pillow; her rosy lips smiled, and little dimples showed in her cheeks; her white soft hands were folded amidst the scented lace and linen of which the bed was made. Gervaise almost forgot to look at the glittering beads hung round her throat, in wondering at her loveliness, but Yolande pulled him by the arm.

"Do not look at her," she whispered softly, "since her beauty has cost dear already; look rather at what remains of those who thought her as fair as you do now; see here," and she pointed with her finger to each bead in turn.

"This was Pierrot, and this Hildebrandt, and these are Adrian, and Sigbert, and Algar, and Cenred, and that is Pharamond, and that Raoul, and last of all here is your own master Prince Florestan. Seek him now where you will and you will not find him, and you shall never see him again till the cord is cut and the charm broken."

"Of what is the cord made?" whispered Gervaise.

"It is of the finest gold," she answered. "Nay, do not you touch her lest she wake. I will show it to you." And Yolande put down the lantern and softly put out her hands to slip the beads aside, but as she did so, her fingers closed around the golden string, and directly she was gone. Another bead was added to the necklace, and Gervaise was alone with the sleeping Princess. He gazed about him in sore amazement and fear. He dared not call lest Fiorimonde should wake.

"Yolande," he whispered as loud as he dared, "Yolande where are you?" but no Yolande answered.

Then he bent down over the Princess and gazed at the necklace. Another bead was strung upon it next to the one to which Yolande had pointed as Prince Florestan. Again he counted them. "Eleven before, now there are twelve. Oh hateful Princess! I know now where go the brave kings and princes who came to woo you, and where, too, is my Yolande," and as he looked at the last bead, tears filled his eyes. It was brighter and clearer than the others, and of a warm red hue, like the red dress Yolande had worn. The Princess turned and laughed in her sleep, and at the sound of her laughter Gervaise was filled with horror and loathing. He crept shuddering from the room, and all night long sat up alone, plotting how he might defeat Fiorimonde, and set Florestan and Yolande free.

"Next morning when Fiorimonde dressed she looked at her necklace and counted its beads, but she was much perplexed, for a new bead was added to the string."—P. 29.

Next morning when Fiorimonde dressed she looked at her necklace and counted its beads, but she was much perplexed, for a new bead was added to the string.

"Who can have come and grasped my chain unknown to me?" she said to herself, and she sat and pondered for a long time. At last she broke into weird laughter.

"At any rate, whoever it was, is fitly punished," quoth she. "My brave necklace, you can take care of yourself, and if any one tries to steal you, they will get their reward, and add to my glory. In truth I may sleep in peace, and fear nothing."

The day passed away and no one missed Yolande. Towards sunset the rain began to pour in torrents, and there was such a terrible thunderstorm that every one was frightened. The thunder roared, the lightning gleamed flash after flash, every moment it grew fiercer and fiercer. The sky was so dark that, save for the lightning's light, nothing could be seen, but Princess Fiorimonde loved the thunder and lightning.

She sat in a room high up in one of the towers, clad in a black velvet dress, and she watched the lightning from the window, and laughed at each peal of thunder. In the midst of the storm a stranger, wrapped in a cloak, rode to the palace door, and the ladies ran to tell the Princess that a new prince had come to be her suitor. "And he will not tell his name," said they, "but says he hears that all are bidden to ask for the hand of Princess Fiorimonde, and he too would try his good fortune."

"Let him come at once," cried the Princess. "Be he prince or knave what care I? If princes all fly from me it may be better to marry a peasant."

So they led the new-comer up to the room where Fiorimonde sat. He was wrapped in a thick cloak, but he flung it aside as he came in, and showed how rich was his silken clothing underneath ; and so well was he disguised, that Fiorimonde never saw that it was Gervaise, but looked at him, and thought she had never seen him before.

"You are most welcome, stranger prince,

who has come through such lightning and thunder to find me," said she.   " Is it true, then, that
you wish to be my suitor ?   What have you
heard of me ?"

" It is quite true, Princess," said Gervaise.
" And I have heard that you are the most beautiful woman in the world."

" And is that true also?" asked the Princess.
" Look at me now, and see."

Gervaise looked at her and in his heart he
said, " It is quite true, oh wicked Princess!
There never was woman as beautiful as you,
and never before did I hate a woman as I hate
you now ;" but aloud he said,

" No, Princess, that is not true; you are very
beautiful, but I have seen a woman who is fairer
than you for all that your skin looks ivory against
your velvet dress, and your hair is like gold."

" A woman who is fairer than I ? " cried
Fiorimonde, and her breast began to heave and
her eyes to sparkle with rage, for never before
had she heard such a thing said.   " Who are
you who dares come and tell me of women
more beautiful than I am ?"

" I am a suitor who asks to be your husband, Princess," answered Gervaise, "but still I
say I have seen a woman who was fairer than
you."

"Who is she—where is she?" cried Fiorimonde, who could scarcely contain her anger.
"Bring her here at once that I may see if you
speak the truth."

"What will you give me to bring her to
you?" said Gervaise. "Give me that necklace
you wear on your neck, and then I will summon
her in an instant;" but Fiorimonde shook her
head.

"You have asked," said she, "for the only
thing from which I cannot part," and then she
bade her maids bring her her jewel-casket,
and she drew out diamonds, and rubies, and
pearls, and offered them, all or any, to Gervaise.
The lightning shone on them and made them
shine and flash, but he shook his head.

"No, none of these will do," quoth he.
"You can see her for the necklace, but for
nothing else."

"Take it off for yourself then," cried Fiori-

monde, who now was so angry that she only
wished to be rid of Gervaise in any way.

" No, indeed," said Gervaise, " I am no tire-
woman, and should not know how to clasp and
unclasp it ;" and in spite of all Fiorimonde could
say or do, he would not touch either her or the
magic chain.

At night the storm grew even fiercer, but
it did not trouble the Princess.   She waited till
all were asleep, and then she opened her bedroom window and chirruped softly to the little
brown bird, who flew down from the roof at her
call.   Then she gave him a handful of seeds as
before, and he grew and grew and grew till he
was as large as an ostrich, and she sat upon his
back and flew out through the air, laughing at
the lightning and thunder which flashed and
roared around her.   Away they flew till they
came to the old witch's cave, and here they
found the witch sitting at her open door catch-
ing the lightning to make charms with.

"Welcome, my dear," croaked she, as Fiorimonde stepped from the bird ; "here is a
night we both love well.   And how goes

the necklace?—right merrily I see. Twelve beads already—but what is that twelfth?" and she looked at it closely.

"Nay, that is one thing I want you to tell me," said Fiorimonde, drying the rain from her golden hair. "Last night when I slept there were eleven, and this morning there are twelve; and I know not from whence comes the twelfth."

"It is no suitor," said the witch, "but from some young maid, that that bead is made. But why should you mind? It looks well with the others."

"Some young maid," said the Princess. "Then, it must be Cicely or Marybel, or Yolande, who would have robbed me of my necklace as I slept. But what care I? The silly wench is punished now, and so may all others be, who would do the same."

"And when will you get the thirteenth bead, and where will he come from?" asked the witch.

"He waits at the palace now," said Fiorimonde, chuckling. "And this is why I have to speak to you;" and then she told the witch of the stranger who had come in the storm, and of how he would not touch her necklace, nor take the cord in his hand, and how he said also that he knew a woman fairer than she.

"Beware, Princess, beware," cried the witch in a warning voice, as she listened. "Why should you heed tales of other women fairer than you? Have I not made you the most beautiful woman in the world, and can any others do more than I? Give no ear to what this stranger says or you shall rue it." But still the Princess murmured, and said she did not love to hear any one speak of others as beautiful as she.

"Be warned in time," cried the witch, "or you will have cause to repent it. Are you so silly or so vain as to be troubled because a Prince says idly what you know is not true? I tell you do not listen to him, but let him be slung to your chain as soon as may be, and then he will speak no more." And then they talked together of how Fiorimonde could make Gervaise grasp the fatal string.

Next morning when the sun rose, Gervaise

started off into the woods, and there he plucked
acorns and haws, and hips, and strung them
on to a string to form a rude necklace. This
he hid in his bosom, and then went back to the
palace without telling any one.

When the Princess rose, she dressed herself
as beautifully as she could, and braided her
golden locks with great care, for this morning
she meant her new suitor to meet his fate.
After breakfast, she stepped into the garden,
where the sun shone brightly, and all looked
fresh after the storm. Here from the grass
she picked up a golden ball, and began to play
with it.

"Go to our new guest," cried she to her
ladies, "and ask him to come here and play at
ball with me." So they went, and soon they
returned bringing Gervaise with them.

"Good morrow, prince," cried she. "Pray,
come and try your skill at this game with me;
and you," she said to her ladies, "do not wait
to watch our play, but each go your way, and
do what pleases you best." So they all went
away, and left her alone with Gervaise.

"Well, prince," cried she as they began to play, "what do you think of me by morning light? Yesterday when you came it was so dark, with thunder and clouds, that you could scarcely see my face, but now that there is bright sunshine, pray look well at me, and see if you do not think me as beautiful as any woman on earth," and she smiled at Gervaise, and looked so lovely as she spoke, that he scarce knew how to answer her; but he remembered Yolande, and said,

"Doubtless you are very beautiful; then why should you mind my telling you that I have seen a woman lovelier than you?"

At this the Princess again began to be angry, but she thought of the witch's words and said,

"Then, if you think there is a woman fairer than I, look at my beads, and now, that you see their colours in the sun, say if you ever saw such jewels before."

"It is true I have never seen beads like yours, but I have a necklace here, which pleases me better;" and from his pocket he drew the haws and acorns, which he had strung together.

"What is that necklace, and where did you get it? Show it to me!" cried Fiorimonde; but Gervaise held it out of her reach, and said,

"I like my necklace better than yours, Princess; and, believe me, there is no necklace like mine in all the world."

"Why; is it a fairy necklace? What does it do? Pray give it to me!" cried Fiorimonde, trembling with anger and curiosity, for she thought, "Perhaps it has power to make the wearer beautiful; perhaps it was worn by the woman whom he thought more beautiful than I, and that is why she looked so fair."

"Come, I will make a fair exchange," said Gervaise. "Give me your necklace and you shall have mine, and when it is round your throat I will truthfully say that you are the fairest woman in the world; but first I must have your necklace."

"Take it, then," cried the Princess, who, in her rage and eagerness, forgot all else, and she

"Then he picked up the necklace on the point of his sword and carried it, slung thereon, into the council chamber."—P. 39.

seized the string of beads to lift it from her
neck, but no sooner had she taken it in her
hands than they fell with a rattle to the earth,
and Fiorimonde herself was nowhere to be seen.
Gervaise bent down over the necklace as it lay
upon the grass, and, with a smile, counted
thirteen beads; and he knew that the thirteenth
was the wicked Princess, who had herself met
the evil fate she had prepared for so many
others.

"Oh, clever Princess!" cried he, laughing
aloud, "you are not so very clever, I think, to
be so easily outwitted." Then he picked up
the necklace on the point of the sword and
carried it, slung thereon, into the council chamber, where sat the King surrounded by states-
men and courtiers busy with state affairs.

"Pray, King," said Gervaise, "send some
one to seek for Princess Fiorimonde. A
moment ago she played with me at ball in the
garden, and now she is nowhere to be seen."

The King desired that servants should seek
her Royal Highness; but they came back saying
she was not to be found.

"Then let me see if I cannot bring her to you; but first let those who have been longer lost than she, come and tell their own tale." And, so saying, Gervaise let the necklace slip from his sword on to the floor, and taking from his breast a sharp dagger, proceeded to cut the golden thread on which the beads were strung and as he clave it in two there came a mighty noise like a clap of thunder.

"Now;" cried he, "look, and see King Pierrot who was lost," and as he spoke he drew from the cord a bead, and King Pierrot, in his royal clothes, with his sword at his side, stood before them.

"Treachery!" he cried, but ere he could say more Gervaise had drawn off another bead, and King Hildebrandt appeared, and after him came Adrian, and Sigbert, and Algar, and Cenred, and Pharamond, and Raoul, and last of the princes, Gervaise's own dear master Florestan, and they all denounced Princess Fiorimonde and her wickedness.

"And now," cried Gervaise, "here is she who has helped to save you all," and he drew

off the twelfth bead, and there stood Yolande
in her red dress; and when he saw her Gervaise
flung away his dagger and took her in his arms,
and they wept for joy.

The King and all the courtiers sat pale
and trembling, unable to speak for fear and
shame. At length the King said with a deep
groan,

"We owe you deep amends, O noble kings
and princes! What punishment do you wish us
to prepare for our most guilty daughter?" but
here Gervaise stopped him, and said,

"Give her no other punishment than what
she has chosen for herself. See, here she is,
the thirteenth bead upon the string; let no one
dare to draw it off, but let this string be hung
up where all people can see it and see the one
bead, and know the wicked Princess is punished
for her sorcery, so it will be a warning to others
who would do like her."

So they lifted the golden thread with great
care and hung it up outside the town-hall, and
there the one bead glittered and gleamed in the
sunlight, and all who saw it knew that it was

the wicked Princess Fiorimonde who had justly met her fate.

Then all the kings and princes thanked Gervaise and Yolande, and loaded them with presents, and each went to his own land.

And Gervaise married Yolande, and they went back with Prince Florestan to their home, and all lived happily to the end of their lives.

ONG ago there lived a wandering musician and his wife, whose names were Arasmon and Chrysea. Arasmon played upon a lute to which Chrysea sang, and their music was so beautiful that people followed them in crowds and gave them as much money as they wanted. When Arasmon played all who heard him were silent from wonder and admiration, but when Chrysea sang they could not refrain from weeping, for her voice was more beautiful than anything they had ever heard before.

Both were young and lovely, and were as happy as the day was long, for they loved each other dearly, and liked wandering about seeing new countries and people and making sweet music. They went to all sorts of places, sometimes to big cities, sometimes to little villages, sometimes to lonely cottages by the sea-shore, and sometimes they strolled along the green lanes and fields, singing and playing so exquisitely, that the very birds flew down from the trees to listen to them.

One day they crossed a dark line of hills, and came out on a wild moorland country, where they had never been before. On the side of the hill they saw a little village, and at once turned towards it, but as they drew near Chrysea said,

"What gloomy place is this? See how dark and miserable it looks."

"Let us try to cheer it with some music," said Arasmon, and began to play upon his lute, while Chrysea sang. One by one the villagers came out of their cottages and gathered round them to listen, but Chrysea thought she had never before seen such forlorn-looking people. They were thin and bent, their faces were pale

"One by one the villagers came out of their cottages, and gathered round them to listen."—ᴘ. 44.

and haggard, also their clothes looked old and
threadbare, and in some places were worn into
holes.   But they crowded about Arasmon and
Chrysea, and begged them to go on playing and
singing, and as they listened the women shed
tears, and the men hid their faces and were
silent.   When they stopped, the people began
to feel in their pockets as if to find some coins,
but Arasmon cried,

"Nay, good friends, keep your money for
yourselves.   You have not too much of it, to
judge by your looks.   But let us stay with you
for to-night, and give us food and lodging, and
we shall think ourselves well paid, and will
play and sing to you as much as you like."

"Stay with us as long as you can, stay with
us always," begged the people; and each one
entreated to be allowed to receive the strangers
and give them the best they had.   So Arasmon
and Chrysea played and sang to them till they
were tired, and at last, when the heavy rain
began to fall, they turned towards the village,
but as they passed through its narrow streets
they thought the place itself looked even sadder

than its inmates. The houses were ill-built, and seemed to be almost tumbling down. The streets were uneven and badly kept. In the gardens they saw no flowers, but dank dark weeds. They went into a cottage which the people pointed out to them, and Arasmon lay down by the fire, calling to Chrysea to rest also, as they had walked far, and she must be weary. He soon fell asleep, but Chrysea sat at the door watching the dark clouds as they drifted over the darker houses. Outside the cottage hung a blackbird in a cage, with drooping wings and scanty plumage. It was the only animal they had yet seen in the village, for of cats or dogs or singing-birds there seemed to be none.

When she saw it, Chrysea turned to the woman of the house, who stood beside her, and said,

"Why don't you let it go? It would be much happier flying about in the sunshine."

"The sun never shines here," said the woman sadly. "It could not pierce through the dark clouds which hang over the village. Besides, we do not think of happiness. It is as much as we can do to live."

"But tell me," said Chrysea, "what is it that makes you so sad and your village such a dreary place? I have been to many towns in my life, but to none which looked like this."

"Don't you know," said the woman, "that this place is spell-bound?"

"Spell-bound?" cried Chrysea. "What do you mean?"

The woman turned and pointed towards the moor. "Over yonder," she said, "dwells a terrible old wizard by whom we are bewitched, and he has a number of little dark elves who are his servants, and these are they who make our village what you see it. You don't know how sad it is to live here. The elves steal our eggs, and milk, and poultry, so that there is never enough for us to eat, and we are half-starved. They pull down our houses, and undo our work as fast as we do it. They steal our corn when it is standing in sheaves, so that we find nothing but empty husks;" and as she ceased speaking the woman sighed heavily.

"But if they do all this harm," said Chrysea,

"why do not some of you go to the moor and drive them away?"

"It is part of the spell," said the woman, "that we can neither hear nor see them. I have heard my grandfather say that in the old time this place was no different to others, but one day this terrible old magician came and offered the villagers a great deal of money if they would let him dwell upon the moor; for before that it was covered with golden gorse and heather, and the country folk held all their merrymakings there, but they were tempted with the gold, and sold it, and from that day the elves have tormented us; and as we cannot see them, we cannot get rid of them, but must just bear them as best we may."

"That is a sad way to speak," said Chrysea. "Cannot you find out what the spell really is and break it?"

"It is a song," said the woman, "and every night they sing it afresh. It is said that if any one could go to the moor between midnight and dawn, and could hear them singing it, and then sing through the tune just as they themselves do, the charm would be broken, and we should be free. But it must be some one who has never taken their money, so we cannot do it, for we can neither see nor hear them."

"But I have not taken their money," said Chrysea. "And there is no tune I cannot sing when I have heard it once. So I will go to the moor for you and break the spell."

"Nay, do not think of such a thing," cried the woman. "For the elves are most spiteful, and you don't know what harm they might do to you, even if you set us free."

Chrysea said no more, but all the evening she thought of what the woman had told her, and still stood looking out into the dismal street. When she went to bed she did not sleep, but lay still till the clock struck one. Then she rose softly, and wrapping herself in a cloak, opened the door and stepped out into the rain. As she passed, she looked up and saw the blackbird crouching in the bottom of its cage. She opened the cage door to let it fly, but still it did not move, so she lifted it out in her hand.

E

"Poor bird!" said she gently; "I wish I could give this village its liberty as easily as I can give you yours," and carrying it with her she walked on towards the moor. It was a large waste piece of land, and looked as though it had been burnt, for the ground was charred and black, and there was no grass or green plant growing on it, but there were some blackened stumps of trees, and to these Chrysea went, and hid herself behind one to wait and see what would come. She watched for a long time without seeing any one, but at last there rose from the ground not far from her a lurid gleam, which spread and spread until it became a large circle of light, in the midst of which she saw small dark figures moving, like ugly little men. The light was now so bright that she could distinguish each one quite plainly, and never before had she seen anything so ugly, for they were black as ink, and their faces were twisted and looked cruel and wicked.

They joined hands, and, forming a ring, danced slowly round, and, as they did so, the ground opened, and there rose up in their centre a tiny village exactly like the spell-bound village, only that the houses were but a few inches high. Round this the elves danced, and then they began to sing. Chrysea listened eagerly to their singing, and no sooner had they done, than she opened her lips and sang the same tune through from beginning to end just as she had heard it.

Her voice rang out loud and clear, and at the sound the little village crumbled and fell away as though it had been made of dust.

The elves stood silent for a moment, and then with a wild cry they all rushed towards Chrysea, and at their head she saw one about three times the size of the others, who appeared to be their chief.

"Come, quickly, let us punish the woman who has dared to thwart us," he cried. "What shall we change her to?"

"A frog to croak on the ground," cried one.

"No, an owl to hoot in the night," cried another.

"Oh, for pity's sake," implored Chrysea, "don't change me to one of these loathsome creatures, so that, if Arasmon finds me, he will spurn me."

"Hear her," cried the chief, "and let her have her will. Let us change her to no bird or beast, but to a bright golden harp, and thus shall she remain, until upon her strings some one shall play our tune, which she has dared to sing."

"Agreed!" cried the others, and all began to dance round Chrysea and to sing as they had sung around the village. She shrieked and tried to run, but they stopped her on every side. She cried, "Arasmon! Arasmon!" but no one came, and when the elves' song was done, and they disappeared, all that was left was a little gold harp hanging upon the boughs of the tree, and only the blackbird who sat above knew what had come of poor Chrysea.

When morning dawned, and the villagers awoke, all felt that some great change had taken place. The heavy cloud which hung above the village had cleared away; the sun shone brightly, and the sky was blue; streams which had been dry for years, were running clear and fresh: and the people all felt strong, and able to work again ; the trees were beginning to bud, and in their branches sang birds, whose voices had not been heard there for many a long year. The villagers looked from one to another and said, "Surely the spell is broken ; surely the elves must have fled ;" and they wept for joy.

Arasmon woke with the first beam of the sun, and finding Chrysea was not there, he rose, and went to seek her in the village, calling, "Chrysea, Chrysea! the sun is up and we must journey on our way ;" but no Chrysea answered, so he walked down all the streets, calling "Chrysea! come, Chrysea!" but no Chrysea came. Then he said,

"She has gone into the fields to look for wild flowers, and will soon be back." So he waited for her patiently, but the sun rose high, the villagers went to their work, and she did not return. At this Arasmon was frightened, and asked every one he met if they had seen her, but each one shook his head and said " No, they had seen nothing of her."

Then he called some of the men together and told them that his wife had wandered away, and he feared lest she might lose herself and go still farther, and he asked them to help him to look for her. So some went one way, and some another, to search, and Arasmon himself walked for miles the whole country round, calling "Chrysea! Chrysea!" but no answer came.

The sun was beginning to set and twilight to cover the land, when Arasmon came on to the moor where Chrysea had met her fate. That, too, was changed. Flowers and grass were already beginning to grow there, and the children of the village, who till now had never dared to venture near it, were playing about it. Arasmon could hear their voices as he came near the tree against which Chrysea had leaned, and on which now hung the golden harp. In the branches above sat the blackbird singing, and Arasmon stopped and listened to its song, and thought he had never heard a bird sing so sweetly before. For it sang the magic song by which Chrysea had broken the elves' spell, the first tune it had heard since it regained its liberty.

"Dear blackbird," said Arasmon, looking up to it, "I wish your singing could tell me where to find my wife Chrysea;" and as he looked up he saw a golden harp hanging upon the branches, and he took it down and ran his fingers over the strings. Never before did harp give forth such music. It was like a woman's voice, and was most beautiful, but so sad that when Arasmon heard it he felt inclined to cry. It seemed to be calling for help, but he could not understand what it said, though each time he touched the strings it cried, "Arasmon, Arasmon, I am here! It is I, Chrysea;" but though Arasmon listened, and wondered at its tones, yet he did not know what it said.

He examined it carefully. It was a beautiful little harp, made of pure gold, and at the top was a pair of golden hands and arms clasped together.

"I will keep it," said Arasmon, "for I never yet heard a harp with such a tone, and when Chrysea comes she shall sing to it."

But Chrysea was nowhere to be found, and at last the villagers declared she must be lost, or herself have gone away on purpose, and that it was vain to seek her farther. At this

Arasmon was angry, and saying that he would seek Chrysea as long as he had life, he left the village to wander over the whole world till he should find her. He went on foot, and took with him the golden harp.

He walked for many, many miles far away from the village and the moor, and when he came to any farmhouses, or met any country people on the road he began to play, and every one thronged round him and stared, in breathless surprise at his beautiful music. When he had done he would ask them, " Have you seen my wife Chrysea ? She is dressed in white and gold, and sings more sweetly than any of the birds of heaven."

But all shook their heads and said, " No, she had not been there ;" and whenever he came to a strange village, where he had not been before, he called, " Chrysea, Chrysea, are you here ?" but no Chrysea answered, only the harp in his hands cried whenever he touched its strings, " It is I, Arasmon! It is I, Chrysea!" but though he thought its notes like Chrysea's voice, he never understood them.

He wandered for days and months and years through countries and villages which he had never known before. When night came and he found himself in the fields alone, he would lie down upon his cloak and sleep with his head resting upon the harp, and if by chance one of its golden threads was touched it would cry, " Arasmon, awake, I am here !" Then he would dream that Chrysea was calling him, and would wake and start up to look for her, thinking she must be close at hand.

One day, towards night, when he had walked far, and was very tired, he came to a little village on a lonely, rocky coast by the sea, and he found that a thick mist had come up, and hung over the village, so that he could barely see the path before him as he walked. But he found his way down on to the beach, and there stood a number of fisherwomen, trying to look through the mist towards the sea, and speaking anxiously.

" What is wrong, and for whom are you watching, good folk ?" he asked them.

" We are watching for our husbands," answered one. " They went out in their boats fishing in the early morning, when it was quite light, and then arose this dreadful fog, and they should have come back long ago, and we fear lest they may lose their way in the darkness and strike on a rock and be drowned."

"I too, have lost my wife Chrysea," cried Arasmon. "Has she passed by here? She had long golden hair, and her gown was white and gold, and she sang with a voice like an angel's."

The women all said, "No, they had not seen her;" but still they strained their eyes towards the sea, and Arasmon also began to watch for the return of the boats.

They waited and waited, but they did not come, and every moment the darkness grew thicker and thicker, so that the women could not see each other's faces, though they stood quite near together.

Then Arasmon took his harp and began to play, and its music floated over the water for miles through the darkness, but the women were weeping so for their husbands, that they did not heed it.

"It is useless to watch," said one. "They cannot steer their boats in such a darkness. We shall never see them again."

"I will wait all night till morning," said another, "and all day next day, and next night, till I see some sign of the boats, and know if they be living or dead," but as she stopped speaking, there rose a cry of "Here they are," and two or three fishing-boats were pushed on to the sand close by where they stood, and the women threw their arms round their husbands' necks, and all shouted for joy.

The fishermen asked who it was who had played the harp; "For," they said, "it was that which saved us. We were far from land, and it was so dark that we could not tell whether to go to left or to right, and had no sign to guide us to shore; when of a sudden we heard the most beautiful music, and we followed the sound, and came in quite safely.

"'Twas this good harper who played while we watched," said the women, and one and all turned to Arasmon, and told him with tears of their gratitude, and asked him what they could do for him, or what they could give him in token of their thankfulness; but Arasmon shook his head and said, "You can do nothing for me, unless you can tell me where to seek my wife Chrysea. It is to find her I am wandering;" and when the women shook their heads, and said again they knew nothing of her, the harp-strings as he touched them cried again,

"Arasmon! Arasmon! listen to me. It is I, Chrysea;" but again no one understood it, and though all pitied him, no one could help him.

Next morning when the mist had cleared away, and the sun was shining, a little ship set sail for foreign countries, and Arasmon begged the captain to take him in it that he might seek Chrysea still farther.

They sailed and sailed, till at last they came to the country for which they were bound; but they found the whole land in confusion, and war and fighting everywhere, and all the people were leaving their homes and hiding themselves in the towns, for fear of a terrible enemy, who was invading them. But no one hurt Arasmon as he wandered on with his harp in his hand, only no one would stop to answer him, when he asked if Chrysea had been there, for every one was too frightened and hurried to heed him.

At last he came to the chief city where the King dwelt, and here he found all the men building walls and fortresses, and preparing to defend the town, because they knew their enemy was coming to besiege it, but all the soldiers were gloomy and low-spirited.

"It is impossible for us to conquer," they said, "for there are three of them to every one of us, and they will take our city and make our King prisoner."

That night as the watchmen looked over the walls, they saw in the distance an immense army marching towards them, and their swords and helmets glittered in the moonlight.

Then they gave the signal, and the captains gathered together their men to prepare them for fighting; but so sure were they of being beaten that it was with difficulty their officers could bring them to the walls.

"It would be better," said the soldiers, "to lay down our arms at once and let the enemy enter, for then we should not lose our lives as well as our city and our wealth."

When Arasmon heard this he sat upon the walls of the town, and began to play upon his harp, and this time its music was so loud and clear, that it could be heard far and wide, and its sound was so exultant and joyous, that when the soldiers heard it they raised their heads, and their fears vanished, and they started forward, shouting and calling that they would conquer or be killed.

Then the enemy attacked the city, but the soldiers within met them with so much force that they were driven back, and had to fly, and the victorious army followed them and drove them quite out of their country, and Arasmon went with them, playing on his harp, to cheer them as they went.

When they knew the victory was theirs, all the captains wondered what had caused their sudden success, and one of the lieutenants said, " It was that strange harper who went with us, playing on his harp. When our men heard it, they became as brave as lions." So the captains sent for Arasmon, but when he came they were astonished to see how worn and thin he looked, and could scarcely believe it was he who had made such wonderful music, for his face had grown thin and pale, and there were gray locks in his hair.

They asked him what he would like to have, saying they would give him whatever he would choose, for the great service he had done them.

Arasmon only shook his head and said,

"There is nothing I want that you can give me. I am seeking the whole world round to find my wife Chrysea. It is many many years since I lost her. We two were as happy as birds on the bough. We wandered over the world singing and playing in the sunshine. But now she is gone, and I care for nothing else."

And the captains looked pityingly at him, for they all thought him mad, and could not understand what the harp said when he played on it again, and it cried,

"Listen, Arasmon! I too am here—I, Chrysea."

So Arasmon left that city, and started again, and wandered for days and months and years.

He came by many strange places, and met with many strange people, but he found no trace of Chrysea, and each day he looked older and sadder and thinner.

At length he came to a country where the King loved nothing on earth so much as music. So fond of it was he, that he had musicians and singers by the score, always living in his palace, and there was no way of pleasing him so well as by sending a new musician or singer. So when Arasmon came into the country, and the people heard how marvellously he played, they said at once, " Let us take him to the King. The poor man is mad. Hear how he goes on asking for his wife ; but, mad or not, his playing will delight the King. Let us take him at once to the palace." So, though Arasmon would have resisted them, they dragged him away to the court, and sent a messenger to the King, to say they had found a poor mad wandering harper, who played music the like of which they had never heard before.

The King and Queen, and all the court, sat feasting when the messenger came in saying that the people were bringing a new harper to play before his majesty.

" A new harper!" quoth he. " That is good hearing. Let him be brought here to play to us at once."

So Arasmon was led into the hall, and up to the golden thrones on which sat the King and Queen. A wonderful hall it was, made of gold and silver, and crystal and ivory, and the courtiers, dressed in blue and green and gold and diamonds, were a sight to see. Behind the throne were twelve young maids dressed in pure white, who sang most sweetly, and behind them were the musicians who accompanied them on every kind of instrument. Arasmon had never in his life seen such a splendid sight.

" Come here," cried the King to him, " and let us hear you play." And the singers ceased singing, and the musicians smiled scornfully, for they could not believe Arasmon's music could equal theirs. For he looked to be in a most sorry plight. He had walked far, and the dust of the roads was on him. His clothes were worn threadbare, and stained and soiled,

F

while his face was so thin and anxious and sad
that it was pitiful to see; but his harp of pure
shining gold was undulled, and untarnished.
He began to play, and then all smiles ceased,
and the women began to weep, and the men
sat and stared at him in astonishment. When
he had done the King started up, and throwing
his arms about his neck, cried, "Stay with me.
You shall be my chief musician. Never before
have I heard playing like yours, and whatever
you want I will give you." But when he heard
this, Arasmon knelt on one knee and said,

"My gracious lord, I cannot stay. I have
lost my wife Chrysea. I must search all over
the world till I find her. Ah! how beautiful she was, and how sweetly she sang; her
singing was far sweeter than even the music of
my harp."

"Indeed!" cried the King. "Then I too
would fain hear her. But stay with me, and I
will send messengers all over the world to seek
her far and near, and they will find her much
sooner than you."

So Arasmon stayed at the court, but he said

" He began to play, and then all smiles ceased."—P. 66.

that if Chrysea did not come soon he must go farther to seek her himself.

The King gave orders that he should be clad in the costliest clothes and have all he could want given to him, and after this he would hear no music but Arasmon's playing, so all the other musicians were jealous, and wished he had never come to the palace. But the strangest thing was that no one but Arasmon could play upon his golden harp. All the King's harpers tried, and the King himself tried also, but when they touched the strings there came from them a strange, melancholy wailing, and no one but Arasmon could bring out its beautiful notes.

But the courtiers and musicians grew more and more angry with Arasmon, till at last they hated him bitterly, and only wanted to do him some harm ; for they said,

"Who is he, that our King should love and honour him before us ? After all, it is not his playing which is so beautiful ; it is chiefly the harp on which he plays, and if that were taken from him he would be no better than the rest of us ;" and then they began to consult together as to how they should steal his harp.

One hot summer evening Arasmon went into the palace gardens, and sat down to rest beneath a large beech-tree, when a little way off he saw two courtiers talking together, and heard that they spoke of him, though they did not see him or know he was there.

"The poor man is mad," said one; "of that there is little doubt, but, mad or not, as long as he plays on his harp the King will not listen to any one else."

"The only way is to take the harp from him," said the other. "But it is hard to know how to get it away, for he will never let it go out of his hands."

"We must take it from him when he is sleeping," said the first.

"Certainly," said the other; and then Arasmon heard them settle how and when they would go to his room at night to steal his harp.

He sat still till they were gone, and then he rose, and grasping it tenderly, turned from the palace and walked away through the garden gates.

"I have lost Chrysea," he said, "and now they would take from me even my harp, the only thing I have to love in all this world, but I will go away, far off where they will never find me," and when he was out of sight, he ran with all his might, and never rested till he was far away on a lonely hill, with no one near to see him.

The stars were beginning to shine though it was not yet dark. Arasmon sat on a stone and looked at the country far and near. He could hear the sheep bells tinkling around him, and far, far off in the distance he could see the city and the palace he had left.

Then he began to play on his harp, and as he played the sheep stopped browsing and drew near him to listen.

The stars grew brighter and the evening darker, and he saw a woman carrying a child coming up the hill.

She looked pale and tired, but her face was very happy as she sat down not far from Arasmon and listened to his playing, whilst she looked eagerly across the hill as if she watched for some one who was coming. Presently she turned and said, "How beautifully you play; I never heard music like it before, but what makes you look so sad? Are you unhappy?"

"Yes," said Arasmon, "I am very miserable. I lost my wife Chrysea many years ago, and now I don't know where she can be."

"It is a year since I have seen my husband," said the woman. "He went to the war a year ago, but now there is peace and he is coming back, and to-night he will come over this hill. It was just here we parted, and now I am come to meet him."

"How happy you must be," said Arasmon. "I shall never see Chrysea again," and as he spoke he struck a chord on the harp, which cried, "O Arasmon, my husband! why do you not know me? It is I, Chrysea."

"Do not say that," continued the woman; "you will find her some day. Why do you sit here? Was it here you parted from her?"

Then Arasmon told her how they had gone to a strange desolate village and rested there for the night, and in the morning Chrysea was gone, and that he had wandered all over the world looking for her ever since.

" I think you are foolish," said the woman; "perhaps your wife has been waiting for you at that village all this time. I would go back to the place where I parted from her if I were you, and wait there till she returns. How could I meet my husband if I did not come to the spot where we last were together ? We might both wander on for ever and never find each other; and now, see, here he is coming," and she gave a cry of joy and ran to meet a soldier who was walking up the hill.

Arasmon watched them as they met and kissed, and saw the father lift the child in his arms, then the three walked over the hill together, and when they were gone he sat down and wept bitterly. "What was it she said ?" he said. " That I ought to go back to the spot where we parted. She will not be there, but I will go and die at the place where I last saw her." So again he grasped his harp and started. He travelled many days and weeks by land and sea, till late one day he came in sight of the hill on which stood the little village. But at first he could not believe that he had come to the right place, so changed did all appear. He stopped and looked around him in astonishment. He stood in a shady lane, the arching trees met over his head. The banks were full of spring flowers, and either side of the hedge were fields full of young green corn.

"Can this be the wretched bare road down which we walked together? I would indeed it were, and that she were with me now," said he. When he looked across to the village, the change seemed greater still. There were many more cottages, and they were trim and well kept, standing in neat gardens full of flowers. He heard the cheerful voices of the peasants, and the laughter of the village children. The whole place seemed to be full of life and happiness. He stopped again upon the mound where he and Chrysea had first played and sung.

"It is many, many a long year since I was here," he said. "Time has changed all things strangely; but it would be hard to say which is the more altered, this village or I, for then it was sunk in poverty and wretchedness, and now it has gained happiness and wealth, and I, who was so happy and glad, now am broken-down and worn. I have lost my only wealth, my wife Chrysea. It was just here she stood and sang, and now I shall never see her again or hear her singing."

There came past him a young girl driving some cows, and he turned and spoke to her. "Tell me, I beg," he said, "is not your village much changed of late years? I was here long ago, but I cannot now think it the same place, for this is as bright and flourishing a town as I have ever seen, and I remember it only as a dreary tumble-down village where the grass never grew."

"Oh!" said the girl, "then you were here in our bad time, but we do not now like to speak of that, for fear our troubles should return. Folks say we were spell-bound. 'Tis so long ago that I can scarcely remember it, for I was quite a little child then. But a wandering musician and his wife set us free; at least, everything began to mend after they came, and now we think they must have been angels from heaven, for next day they went, and we have never seen them since."

"It was I and my wife Chrysea," cried Arasmon. "Have you seen her? Has she been here? I have sought all over the world ever since, but I cannot find her, and now I fear lest she be dead."

The girl stared at him in surprise. "You? you poor old man! Of what are you talking? You must surely be mad to say such things. These musicians were the most beautiful people upon the earth, and they were young and dressed in shining white and gold, and you are old and gray and ragged, and surely you are very ill too, for you seem to be so weak that you can scarcely walk. Come home with me, and I will give you food and rest till you are better."

Arasmon shook his head. "I am seeking Chrysea," he said, "and I will rest no more till I have found her;" and the girl, seeing that he was determined, left him alone and went on her way driving her cows before her.

When she had gone Arasmon sat by the wayside and wept as though his heart would break. "It is too true," he said; "I am so old and worn that when I find her she will not know me," and as he again fell a-weeping his hand struck the harp-strings, and they cried, "I have watched you through all these years, my Arasmon. Take comfort, I am very near," and his tears ceased, and he was soothed by the voice of the harp, though he knew not why.

Then he rose. "I will go to the moor," he said, "and look for the tree on which I found my harp, and that will be my last resting-place, for surely my strength will carry me no farther." So he tottered slowly on, calling, as he went, in a weak voice, "Chrysea, my Chrysea! are you here? I have sought you over the world since you left me, and now that I am old and like to die, I am come to seek you where we parted."

When he came upon the moor, he wondered again at the change of all the country round. He thought of the charred, blackened waste on which he had stood before, and now he looked with amazement at the golden gorse, the purple heather, so thick that he could scarcely pick his way amongst it.

"It is a beautiful place now," he said, "but I liked it better years ago, deserted and desolate though it was, for my Chrysea was here."

There were so many trees upon the common that he could not tell which was the one on which his harp had hung, but, unable to go any farther, he staggered and sank down beneath a large oak-tree, in whose branches a blackbird was singing most sweetly. The sun was setting just as of yore when he had found his harp, and most of the birds' songs were over, but this one bird still sang sweet and clear, and Arasmon, tired and weak though he was, raised his head and listened.

"I never heard bird sing like that," he said. "What is the tune it sings? I will play it on my harp before I die." And with what strength remained to him he reached forth his trembling hand, and grasping his harp struck upon it the notes of the bird's song, then he fell back exhausted, and his eyes closed.

At once the harp slid from his hand, and

Chrysea stood beside him—Chrysea dressed as of old, in shining white and gold, with bright hair and eyes.

"Arasmon!" she cried, "see, it is I, Chrysea!" but Arasmon did not move. Then she raised her voice and sang more sweetly than the bird overhead, and Arasmon opened his eyes and looked at her.

"Chrysea!" cried he; "I have found my wife Chrysea!" and he laid his head on her bosom and died. And when Chrysea saw it her heart broke, and she lay beside him and died without a word.

In the morning when some of the villagers crossed the common they saw Arasmon and Chrysea lying beneath the oak-tree in each other's arms, and drew near them, thinking they were asleep, but when they saw their faces they knew they were dead.

Then an old man stooped and looked at Chrysea, and said,

"Surely it is the woman who came to us and sang long ago, when we were in our troubles; and, though he is sadly changed and worn, it is like her husband who played for her singing."

Then came the girl who had driven the cows and told them how she had met Arasmon, and all he had said to her.

"He searched everywhere for his wife, he said," said she. "I am glad he has found her. Where could she be?"

"Would that we had known it was he," said they all, "how we would have greeted him! but see, he looks quite content and as if he wished nothing more, since he has found his wife Chrysea."

ONG ago, in the days of fairies, there lived a King and Queen, who were rich and happy.

But the Queen was a proud, haughty woman, and disliked every one more powerful than herself. And most of all, she hated the fairy folk, and could not bear them to come to the castle where she and the King dwelt.

Time passed, and the Queen had a little baby,—a daughter whom they called Joan— and the bells were rung, and there were great rejoicings all over the country, and the King and Queen were happy as the day is long.

One day as the Queen sat by the cradle of

the little Princess, watching it, she said, " My
pretty babe, when you are grown to be a woman
you will be rich and beautiful, and you shall
marry some young Prince, who will love you
dearly, and then in your turn be Queen, and
have a fine palace, and jewels, and lands to
your heart's content."   Scarcely had she done
speaking when she heard a little noise beside
her, and, looking up, saw a woman dressed
in yellow from head to foot standing on the
other side of the cradle.   She wore a yellow
cap, which covered her head completely, so
that no hair was seen, and her eyes, which
looked cunning and fierce, were yellow as her
dress.

"And how do you know, Queen, that your
child will be so happy ?   Whose help will you
seek to get her all these fine things ?" said the
strange woman.

"I will ask no one's help," said the Queen
haughtily, "for I am Queen of the land, and can
have what I please."

The yellow woman laughed, and said,
" Don't be too sure, proud Queen ; but the next

night that the moon is bright, guard well the Princess when the clock strikes twelve, lest aught of her's be stolen from her."

" No thief shall come near her," cried the Queen; but ere she had done speaking the woman had vanished, and the Queen knew it was a fairy.

The sky that night was dark and overcast, and no moon to be seen, and the next night was the same, but the third night the moon shone bright and clear, and as the clock struck twelve the Queen awoke and looked at the baby, who was sleeping peacefully in its cradle ; but 'twixt the strokes of the clock she heard a faint whistling outside the window, which grew louder and fuller each moment. 'Twas as if some one whistled to decoy away a bird, and on hearing it the baby awoke and began to cry bitterly. The Queen could not quiet her, try how she might. At last the little one gave one scream louder than all the others and then lay quite still, and at that moment the Queen saw something flutter across the room like a tiny bird, with pink, soft feathers. It flew straight

G

out of the window, and the whistling ceased, and all again was quiet as before.   The Queen took the baby in her arms and looked at it anxiously by the light of the moon, but it looked well and slept calmly, so its mother placed it in its cradle and tried to forget the yellow fairy and the whistling.

The nurse of the Princess Joan was a very wise old woman who knew a great deal of fairies and their ways, and as the child grew up she watched her with an anxious face.

"She is under a charm," she said, "though what it is I don't know; but before she is a woman they will see how different she is from others."

The nurse's words proved to be true.   No one had ever seen a little girl like the Princess. Nothing troubled her.   She never shed one tear.   If she were angry she would stamp her feet and her eyes would flash, but she never wept, and she loved nobody.   When her little dog died she laughed outright; when the King her father went to the war it did not grieve her; and when he returned she was no happier than she had been when he was away. She never kissed her mother, or her ladies, and when they said they loved her, she stared at them, and asked what they meant. At this the ladies were angry with her and chid her for being hard-hearted, but the old nurse always stopped them, saying,

"'Tis not her you should blame. She is enchanted, but 'tis not her fault."

Princess Joan grew up and was the loveliest woman in the land. It was many long years since any one so fair had been seen, but for all that her mother mourned over her sorely, and her eyes were red with crying for her beautiful daughter, who had never yet wept one tear herself.

The neighbouring country was governed by a King and Queen who had only one son, named Michael, whom everybody loved dearly. He was a handsome young man, and as good as he was handsome. He was as gracious to the poorest beggar as to the greatest lord, and all the poor folk came to him to tell him their troubles, if they thought they were badly treated;

and because he was brave and handsome also, the court people loved him as well as the peasants.

In this country there stood on a high hill a round tower, and at the top of it lived an old wizard. No man knew his age, for he had dwelt there for hundreds of years, and no one knew how the tower had been built, for it was made of one huge stone, and there were no joins in it at all.

The King and Queen were afraid of the old magician, and never went near him ; indeed, no one in all the country had ever ventured to climb the tower and see the old man at his work except Prince Michael, who knew the old sorcerer well and did not fear him at all, but went up and down the tower as he chose.

One bright moonlight night it chanced that the Prince found himself alone on the hill-side, and seeing a bright light shining from the top of the tower he resolved to enter and pay the old man a visit. So he went to a little door, and pushing it open stepped into a narrow, dark, winding staircase, that went straight up the centre to the room at the top, in which the wizard dwelt. The staircase was pitch dark, for there were no windows. Moreover, it was so narrow that only one person could walk in it at a time, but Prince Michael knew the way quite well, and climbed and climbed till he saw a chink of light, and at last trod through a little doorway into the room in which the sorcerer sat.

This room was as light as day, for it was lit by a lamp which the old man himself had made, and in which no oil or wick was burning, but every day it was filled with sunbeams, and held them at night after the sun had set.

So the whole room was brilliant, and in the middle sat the wizard, who was a wonderful old man to look on, for he was all white. His beard was white as snow, and from afar you could not tell which was beard and which gown, but when you came near you saw that the beard flowed nearly to his feet, and his skin was as white as either beard or gown. And his eyes were quite colourless, but as bright as two candles.

When Michael entered he sat looking at an enormous book full of coloured pictures of little men and women about three inches high each. They were not like other pictures, for they walked and moved over the page as though they were alive.

" It is I, father.   What book are you looking at ?" said Michael, stepping up to the old man's side.

" In this book," said the wizard, " I keep the portraits of all the men and women in the world, and they are living portraits too, for they move, and look just like the originals."

" That must be very amusing," cried Michael. " Pray show me the portraits of all the Kings, and Queens, and Princesses. This will be delightful," and he knelt down by the old man and looked over his shoulder.

The sorcerer muttered to himself and turned over the pages, and then stopped at one on which Michael saw little figures of Kings and Queens of all sorts, some of which he knew, and some of which he had never seen before.

" There," he cried, " is old King Réné who

"'Tis their daughter, Princess Joan," said the wizard with a sigh. "But do not look at her, my son, for she will bring nothing but trouble to all who know her."—P. 87.

came to our court last year, and that is Queen
Constance, and that is their nephew Prince
Guilbert, who will be king when they are dead,
and here are our neighbours the King and
Queen of the next country, and oh, my father,
who is this lovely Princess next to them ?"

"'Tis their daughter Princess Joan," said
the wizard with a sigh. " But do not look at
her, my son, for she will bring nothing but
trouble to all who know her."

" I don't care if she bring trouble or happiness," cried the Prince. " But for certain she
is the most beautiful creature in the world," and
he seized the book and looked long at the tiny
figure of the Princess. Truly it was very beautiful. It was dressed in white, with a golden
girdle round the waist, and a wreath of golden
daisies on its head, and as Michael looked, it
turned upon the pages, and smiled at him till he
smiled back again, and could not move his eyes
from it.

When the wizard saw this, he took the book
from the young man's hands, and hid it away,
saying,

" Think no more of Princess Joan, however beautiful she be, or one day you will rue it dearly."

Prince Michael made no answer, but he thought all the more of the little picture of the Princess.   After he had left the tower, and returned to the palace, he could not forget her, but dreamt of her all night, and thought of her all day.

Next morning he went to the King and said, " My father, I am come to beg that you will send to the King of the next country and ask if I may have his daughter, Princess Joan, for my wife, for I have seen her portrait, and there is no one in the world whom I love so well."

When the King heard this he was delighted.

" Our good neighbours," he said, " are rich and powerful, and it will be a capital thing for our son to marry their daughter."   So he at once sent off an ambassador to beg for the hand of Princess Joan for Prince Michael.

Joan's father and mother were delighted with the offer, and at once resolved to accept it ; but the Queen's heart sank within her, for she thought, "Our poor Joan is not like any other maid who ever lived before, and perhaps when Prince Michael sees her and finds this out, he will refuse to wed her after all;" but she said nothing of her fears, and the ambassador returned to the court, loaded with presents, and bearing a message of acceptance.

Till his return Prince Michael knew no peace or rest, but wandered about among the hills by himself, thinking of Joan, and still, in his heart, he wondered what the magician had meant when he said that if he thought much of Princess Joan, one day he would rue it.

At last he said to himself, " I will disguise myself as a poor man, and go and see my Princess for myself before the ambassador returns, then shall I know what the wizard means."

So he dressed himself as a peasant, and started alone without telling any one whither he went, and he travelled day and night till he came to the country where Joan dwelt and to her father's palace. Then he walked near the palace gardens, and no one noticed him, and he saw a group of lovely ladies, who sat together on the grass.

His heart beat high as he looked at them, for in their midst, most beautiful of all, sat the Princess Joan. Her yellow hair fell to her waist, her face was like a blush rose, and her eyes were blue as forget-me-nots, but when she lifted them, he saw that they were clear and hard as glass, and her voice when she spoke was like a bright cold bell.

There ran up to her a little serving-maid, crying bitterly, and said,

"I beg of you, Princess, to let me return to my own home for a time, for my father, the huntsman, has broken his leg and is very ill."

"Why should you cry for that?" said the Princess. "'Tis your father and not you that is hurt; but you may go, for when you cry and your eyes look red you are ugly, and I don't like to see you, so be sure that when you return you are pretty and bright as ever."

When her ladies heard her they looked angry, but no one spoke, and the little maid went crying away.

Up there came a groom from the palace and said,

"Your Royal Highness, the horse that you rode yesterday is dead, and we think it is because you would ride so far when it was already tired, as we told you."

"Dead is it?" cried the Princess. "Then see quickly and get me another, that I may ride again to-morrow, and be sure this time that it is a good strong horse, or it may give way beneath me and so my ride be shortened."

The groom went away muttering, and the Princess's ladies looked even graver than before, but the Princess's own face was bright as a summer sky, and she talked on without heeding their sad looks.

Prince Michael turned away with a heavy heart.

"The magician spoke truly," he said to himself, "and there will be nothing but sorrow for all those who love my poor Princess Joan."

Yet he could not bear to leave her and return at once to his own home, and still he remained near the palace. and for some days watched her unnoticed, when she walked and rode, and listened to all she said, and each day he grieved more and more, for she never said one kind loving word to any one; yet each day when he saw how beautiful she was he loved her more and more.

When he again returned to his own home he found great rejoicings everywhere, for the ambassador had returned with a message from Joan's father promising she should marry the Prince, and everywhere preparations were being made for the entry of the Princess to her new home.

"And now, my son," said the King, "all is arranged for you to journey in state to her father's court and bring back your bride, so now I hope that you are happy and wish for nothing more."

On hearing this Prince Michael's face was sad and grave, and his father and mother wondered what ailed him. But he said to himself, "I will never marry my Joan till she loves me as I do her, and how can she ever do that when she loves no one, not even her own father and mother?"

At the court of Joan's father grand preparations had been made, and all was in excitement
when Prince Michael arrived with servants, and
horses, and presents for the bride.

The King and Queen sat in state to receive
him, and beside them was Joan, and she looked
so beautiful, in a dress as blue as her eyes, that
every one said, " How glad he will be when he
sees how lovely she is."

· There was a blowing of trumpets and ringing
of bells when Prince Michael, followed by his
attendants, entered, and the King and Queen
and all the courtiers rose.

He passed up the hall to the thrones on
which they sat, and kneeling on one knee, kissed
their hands, and last he kissed the hand of the
Princess, but he did not lift his eyes from the
ground or look in her face, and his own was so
sad that the people whispered to each other, and
said, " What is the matter, and why does he
look so unhappy ?   Surely he ought to be content when he sees how beautiful she is."

At night when the merrymakings were over
the Prince sent a message to the Queen,

begging she would speak with him alone, and when she heard this her heart sank, and she thought, " He must know that there is something amiss with Joan, and perhaps he comes to say he will not marry her after all."

So she sent every one away, except the old nurse and bid the Prince to come.

When he came in and saw her sad looks he said, "You have guessed then, Queen, why I come to speak to you. Tell me truly what ails Princess Joan, and why is she unlike any one I ever saw." The Queen cried bitterly, and said, "I know not; would I did!" but the old nurse said,

" I know and will tell you, Prince. Princess Joan is under a spell. A bad fairy enchanted her when she was a tiny baby, and till this charm is broken, she will never be like other people."

"And what is the charm?" asked the Prince.

"Nay, that I don't know," said the nurse. Then she told Michael of the yellow woman and the whistling the Queen had heard at night;

and as he listened the Prince sighed and said,
" There is no charm which cannot be broken if
one does but know how, but this is hard to do,
for we do not know what the spell is, or who is
the fairy who cast it.   But bid the people cease
their preparations, Queen, and stop the wedding
rejoicings, for there will be no wedding.   No,
not till I have found the fairy who has wronged
my Joan, and made her set her free.   To-morrow
I shall start at break of day, and journey to the
farthest ends of the world, to search for what
can break the charm.   But I pray, Queen, that
Joan may wait for me for seven years, and if,
when they are past, I have not returned, and
you have heard nothing of me, you must think
that I am dead and gone, and marry her to
whom you will, for if I be alive, I will return
before then.   And till seven years are past
remember that Joan is still mine."

On hearing this the Queen wept still more,
and begged the Prince either to remain and
marry Joan, or to leave her and return to his
home and forget her ; but if he wandered away
to lands of goblins and fairies, no one would

know what had become of him, and he would
never find the fairy who had charmed Joan or
learn how to break the spell; but Prince Michael
only shook his head, and said, "I have sworn
that I will not marry Joan till she loves me as I
do her, neither can I return to my home and
forget her, so bid her be ready at dawn to-
morrow to bid me farewell, and tell none that I
am going till I have gone. Also I beg you
to send a messenger to my father and mother
to tell them why I do not return, for I will
not see them first, lest they too should try to
dissuade me." The Queen said no more, but
she cried very bitterly ; but the old nurse smiled
and nodded to Michael and said,

"You do well. You are a noble Prince, and
would well deserve our Princess's love."

Next morning at break of day the Queen
awoke the Princess and bade her rise, for Prince
Michael waited to bid her good-bye. The
Prince stood at the door of the palace, and
when Princess Joan came out looking lovelier
than ever in the dim morning light, the tears
filled his eyes, and he thought, "Most likely I

shall never see her again, and then she will never know how much I have loved her."

"Good-bye, Joan," he said; "do not quite forget me for seven years, for perhaps I may yet come back and marry you."

"And why do you go?" said Joan; "I had thought there would be a grand wedding, and I should have all the gifts that are being pre-pared for me, and now I shall have nothing; but good-bye, if go you must."

Michael sighed as he mounted his horse and bade her farewell. When he looked back at the palace, the Queen and Joan still stood at the door, and the Queen sobbed; but Princess Joan looked quite happy and contented, and smiled brightly.

Prince Michael rode and rode, till he came to his own home, and then he turned at once to the tower in which dwelt the magician. He climbed the tower and found the old man sitting alone as before, but he had no book before him, and he looked very grave.

"I know why you are come," he said, as soon as Michael entered the room. "So you

H

have seen Princess Joan; and do you still wish to marry her?"

"I will marry her, or no one," said Michael. "But not till I have found out who has bewitched her, and have broken the charm."

"You will have to search far for that," said the wizard; "And it may be years ere you could set her free. Forget her, my son, and return to your own home, and do not waste your life in a fruitless quest."

"I will seek to break the charm, even if it take my whole life," said Michael. "But tell me what it is, and how shall I find out how to break it."

"A fairy has stolen her heart," said the wizard, "and that is why she loves no one, and can feel no sorrow; she has no heart with which to love or pity, and till it is found and restored to her, she will be hard and cold as stone. The fairy swore she would be revenged on her mother for her pride, and so she is."

"Then I will go and seek her heart, and bring it back to her," said Michael. "But

where shall I look for it ? Tell me at least where
has the fairy hidden it."

" She has taken it to a castle in which are
kept all the hearts of men and women, that
fairies steal, or that they themselves throw
away; and this castle is very far from here;
moreover, it is guarded by an old gnome,
who is spiteful and cruel, and who pays no
heed to those who beg him to let them enter.
Give up the Princess and return to your home,
for if you go, you will only die, or be enchanted
like poor Princess Joan."

" Nevertheless, I shall go," said Michael.
" So tell me what path to take, and I will start
at once."

On hearing this the sorcerer took from his
bosom a small round piece of glass, and gave it
to the young man. " Take this," he said ; "It is
all that I can give you, to help you, and through
it you must look at the stars, and you will see
that they are all of different colours—blue,
green, red, and yellow ; look for the one which
is the deepest, brightest red, and follow it ; it
will lead you many miles both by land and sea,

but follow steadily, and let nothing turn you from your course, and you will surely come to the castle wherein is imprisoned the heart of your Princess."

The Prince thanked the magician, and took the glass; then bidding him "Good-bye," he left the strangely lighted chamber, and went down the dark staircase, and stood again on the hill outside, with the dark sky overhead filled with shining stars.

Michael raised the glass and looked at them through it, and then he almost shouted with surprise, for they looked wonderful. They were like jewels of all colours—green, blue, yellow, pink—and in the south was one of a deep glowing red, like a blood-red rose, and Michael knew that that was the star he must follow.

Then he looked back towards his father's palace. "Farewell," he said; "some day I will return, and bring with me my Princess Joan." So he set off, and journeyed and journeyed, till he had reached towns and villages which he had never seen before. All that night he travelled while the stars shone, and he could see

the rosy star to follow. But when the stars
grew pale, and the sun rose, and people began
to wake up and turn to their work, he lay down
under a tree and slept soundly. When he
woke the day was almost done, and the sun
was sinking. So he went to a little town near
and bought food, and rested till again the stars
shone in the sky. Then he rose and went on all
night, still following the crimson star. So passed
many days and nights, and he journeyed through
strange lands, and his heart sank when he
thought, " So may I wander all round the world,
and come no nearer to the star, or to the castle
where they keep the heart of my poor Joan."

At last he came to the sea-shore, and in
front of him lay a great cold sea, and beyond it
he saw no sign of land. But the star shone
right over it, and he knew that he must cross,
if he still would follow it. It was in the evening, the sun had set, but some fishermen still
remained on the beach, resting beside their
boats. Michael went up to them, and taking
some money from his pocket, asked for how
much they would sell him one of their boats.

At this the men looked surprised, and one of them said, "Why do you wish to buy a boat? We use them to fish near the shore, but no boat or ship has ever crossed this sea, for no one knows what land is beyond."

"Then I will be the first to find out," said Michael. "Tell me how much you want, and give me your largest boat." On this the men muttered together, and one said, "He is mad." "Yes," said another, "but his money is good, for all that. Let the madman have his way. It will hurt him, not us." So they gave Michael their best boat, and he paid them well, and he set sail and steered where the red star shone. He sailed all night till he had left every trace of land behind him, and saw no shore in front, only the cold, gray sea on every side. By day he kept the boat still, afraid lest he should get out of the track of the star, but when the second night came he was so weary that in spite of himself he fell asleep. When he awoke he found the sun had risen, and his boat was drifting close to land. It was a flat, lonely shore, without trees or grass growing in sight, and facing him was an immense castle. It was built of black marble, and a more gloomy place could not be, for the windows were small and high up, and were all barred across, with heavy iron bars, and the castle had no spires or towers, but was one square black block, and looked more like a prison than a castle. Around it was a high wall, and outside this a moat, without a bridge.

Michael steered his boat to shore, and stepped from it, and looked about for some way by which he could cross the moat, and try for entrance to the castle. Then he saw a little hut near, and beside it lay an old man apparently fast asleep. He was small and dark, and his face was gray and wrinkled as a monkey's, and he had no hair on his head. Close beside him coiled up was a large snake, also asleep. Michael stood watching them both, afraid to wake them, when, without a word, the gray man raised his head, and opening a pair of dull, gray eyes, fixed them on him. Still he did not speak, and at last the Prince, growing impatient, went up to him and said,

"Friend, I beg you to tell me how I am to enter the castle; or if you have the key, to give it to me."

On this the old man answered, "I have the key, and no one can enter without my leave. What will you give me for it?"

"Why," said Michael, "I have nothing but money," and he took some coins from his pocket as he spoke.

At this the old man laughed. "Your money is nothing to me," he said; "But look yonder. Over there I am building a wall of heavy stones, and I am old, and my strength fails me; stay and work for me at that wall, and in return I will give you the key of the castle."

"But how long must I work?" said Michael, "For unless I can enter the castle before seven years are over, it will be no use to me.

"Look at that serpent," said the old man; "It is sitting on its eggs. When they are hatched you shall have the key and open the castle door. Till then you must be my slave."

"Gladly," said Michael, who was delighted;
"for no snake could take seven years hatching
its eggs."

Then the old man rose, and beckoning to
him to follow, went into the little cottage.
From a nail upon the wall he took a pair of
manacles fastened together by a heavy iron
chain. These he slipped over Michael's wrists,
and stooping down over them, muttered a few
words, and at once the manacles fastened together as if they had been locked, and Michael
could not move them, or draw out his hands.
Then the old man took down another heavy
chain and passed it over the first and fastened
it with more iron rings to his ankles, so that he
could only move his arms and hands a little
way, and could not raise them high, and could
only walk with slow careful steps. This done,
he pointed to where, on the wall high up, hung
a gleaming golden sword, the handle of which
was set with precious stones.

"That," said he, "is the key of the castle,
and you need only push the doors with its point
and they will all fly open; but while your hands

are chained you cannot reach it to lift it down, but when the serpent's eggs are hatched your iron rings will fall off, and you yourself may take the sword down from its place, and push your way into the castle. Now get you to your work, and work hard, or you may rue it."

Then he showed Michael how he was to move the heavy stones, and where to build with them, and he himself sat down by the serpent and watched him, while the Prince went to work with a light heart, for he thought, "It is hard work while it lasts, but 'twill not be for long, and 'tis not much to do to win my Joan." So he worked hard till the sun had set, and then the old man rose, saying, "Enough," and called him into the hut and gave him food and drink, but he ate nothing himself, and then he showed him where he could sleep in one corner, and Michael lay down and slept soundly and dreamed of Joan.

At break of day he was waked by the old man, who again gave him plenty to eat, and again ate nothing, but what he gave to him he took from an urn in the corner, and when

he had done he put into the urn the fragments
that were left.

All day Michael worked hard, and in the
evening as he passed by the snake, he looked at
it as it lay coiled over its eggs, and said,

" How soon will your work be done, and
mine also, good snake? Make haste, I pray,
that I may find my way into the castle, and
return to my Princess."

So the days passed. Each morning the old
man awoke Michael and gave him food, and
set him to work, and all day he laboured
hard. Then when night approached, he called
" Enough," and beckoning him into the hut,
gave him plenty to eat and drink, but never
ate himself, and beside that one word never
spoke, but crouched all day beside the snake,
with closed eyes as if asleep.

Meantime, the doors of the castle never
opened, and no one was seen going in, or
coming out; but sometimes, towards night,
strange noises might be heard from within its
walls; sometimes there were wails and moans,
which it filled Michael with horror to hear, and

sometimes there was sweet singing, so sweet that it drew tears to his eyes.

But the days passed, and the serpent never moved from its eggs, and Michael's heart began to be oppressed with fear, lest the old man was deceiving him, and they should never be hatched at all. As each day passed, he put aside a stone on a bare rock, and one day when he counted over the stones to see how many days were gone, he found that more than a year had passed since his boat had brought him to the shore. His hands had grown hard and brown and cracked, with working at the heavy stones, and his face and neck were blistered and sunburnt with the fierce sun that beat upon them as he worked. His clothes were cut and torn and soiled, and yet he seemed to be no nearer entering the castle. Then he rose and went into the cottage, and looked longingly at the sword which hung high up, on the walls, and raised his arms to try and reach it, but the chains held him down, and as he turned from it in despair he saw the old man standing in the doorway watching him with his cold dull eyes.

"What would you do here?" he asked; "have I not bid you serve me till the serpent's eggs are hatched, and then the sword shall be yours?"

"And when will the serpent's eggs be hatched?" cried Michael in despair.

"That," said the old man, "I cannot tell, but a bargain is a bargain; keep you your part and I will keep mine." Then he turned again to where the serpent lay, and lying down beside it closed his eyes, and Michael returned to his work mournfully.

Time passed, but there came no change. Michael despaired in his heart, but he could not have escaped even if he would, because of the chains which hung from his arms.

"I will work here," he said, "till the seven years are out, then I will climb on the wall which I have built and throw myself into the sea and end my troubles."

Sometimes at night he would take from his bosom the piece of magic glass which the wizard had given him and would gaze through it at the star which still looked a bright crimson colour.

"Why have you led me here, cruel star," he asked sadly, "if you cannot help me more? Are you shining over my home and my Princess, and does she remember me? The seven long years will soon be passed, and they will wed her to another king, and it will be all of no avail that I have given up everything to find her heart, since I have only broken my own."

So the time passed. Michael worked hard by day, but by night he lay and wept. One day, when the seven years had nearly worn themselves away, he bent over a pool of water, and in it saw his own form, and he saw that his hair was thin and streaked with gray, and his face furrowed and seamed, and his eyes dim with crying, also his shoulders were bowed with hard work, and his clothes, once so gorgeous, now hung mere rags upon his bent form.

"Now all is in vain," said he, "for if even I returned to my own home no one will know me, so changed am I. I will go and kill the snake that has caused my misery, and then I will slay the old man who has deceived me."

So he went up to the snake, who lay

motionless coiled over its eggs as usual, and
reached out his hand to grasp its throat, but as
he did so his tears fell and dropped upon its
head, and it writhed fearfully and then glided
away so fast that he could not see where it
went, and left the heap of gray eggs bare beneath his hand.   The old man lay beside them
as still as usual, and did not move or open his
eyes, even when the snake glided hissing past
him.

"If the snake has escaped me," cried
Michael, "then at least I can destroy the
eggs;" and lifting his heel he struck them with
all his might, but his foot left no mark upon
them, nor even moved them from their place.
They might have been made of iron, and each
one nailed to the ground, so hard and firm they
stood.

Michael burst out weeping afresh.   "How
foolish I am," he said, "Yes, and wicked too.
It is not the fault of the poor snake that its
eggs are not hatched.   Perhaps it is enchanted
like me, and waits as patiently for them;" and
he bent his head till his tears fell upon the eggs.

No sooner did they touch them, than the shells broke, and the pieces fell asunder, and from each egg came a small moving thing, though what it was Michael did not see, for he leaped to his feet with a shout of joy, which filled the air, and echoed again from the castle. At this the old man opened his eyes, and raising himself gazed, as if thunderstruck, with astonishment at the eggs.

"'Tis a miracle," he cried, chuckling with joy.

But out of the eggs, there came no one fully formed animal, but from one egg came a foot, from another a leg, from another a tail, and from one a head, and each looked as though it belonged to some different beast, yet all these drew themselves together, and joined so well that the join was not to be seen. And they made a hideous monster of many colours. Then the manacles on Michael's wrists burst asunder, and the chains fell to the ground.

"Now," he cried, "I will go and take for myself the sword from the wall, and win my way into the castle, and nothing shall hinder me more." And he turned and rushed into the hut. There, upon the wall hung the shining sword, and Michael reached out his hand and seized it firmly, and drew it down from its place.

"I will swear a vow," he cried, "upon this sword, that when I enter the castle, I will say not one word for good or for ill to any one, save to ask for what I come to seek, lest I should again be kept for years. Moreover, I will not taste food or drink, till I have found the heart of my Joan to take back to her." Then, with the sword in his hand, he passed the old man, who still sat chuckling over the monster, too busy to heed him, and he went straight on to the bridgeless moat. It was not wide, and he swam it easily, and scrambled up the bank by the stone wall. He pushed with the point of the sword at the gate, and it at once flew open, and he stood in the outer court. Then he saw a heavy door in the wall of the castle, and went up to it, nothing fearing, and, on touching it with the sword's point, it too flew open at once, and he entered.

He stepped into a passage filled with flowers and hung with silken hangings. He trod upon a velvet carpet, and the air was laden with sweet scents, and from afar he heard sweet voices singing. He strode on through another door, and yet another, and at each step he took all things became lovelier, till at last he passed into a splendid chamber, the like of which he had never seen before. In the ceiling were precious stones set in patterns of flowers and crowns, on the walls were soft velvet hangings and embroideries. The furniture was of carven gold and silver and ivory, and everywhere grew flowers of wonderful beauty, which sprang from the floor and crept along the walls, and filled the air with sweet scents, and hanging on the walls were cages which held what Michael thought were birds, which sang most sweetly.

On a table in the centre of the room was a banquet all laid ready, and as Michael looked at it and wondered where he should go farther, a curtain was drawn aside, and there stepped forth a stately dame dressed in black velvet, who came smiling towards him and held out her hand, saying, " I am indeed glad to see you, I am mistress of this castle, and you are very welcome ; but I beg that before you tell me from where you come and what you seek, you will sit down and share this feast with me." Michael was beginning to answer, when he felt the sword in his hand, and remembered his oath, and looking full in the face of the new-comer, said, " I seek the heart of Princess Joan."

" And you shall find it," answered the grand lady. " But first you must rest and eat, for you must be both tired and hungry ;" and so saying she sat at one end of the table, and signed to Michael to sit at the other, and took the golden covers from the dishes, and prepared to begin the feast. Michael knew not what to do, but he sat at the table in silence, and all at once bethought him of the magic glass in his bosom, and drawing it forth when she was not looking, gazed through it at her, and then he beheld no finely-dressed lady, but a wizened old woman, robed in yellow, with an evil yellow face and evil yellow eyes. He

hid the glass again, and sat still as stone, though
the yellow woman pressed on him the different
dishes again and again.   He saw that her face
grew white with rage.   Then all of a sudden she
disappeared, and the lights went out, and he
was left alone in the darkness.   He rose and
searched for the door by which he had entered,
but could not find it nor any way out of the
room ; so there he was, a prisoner alone with
the singing-birds,

"Never mind," quoth he to himself cheerily ;
"I have at last reached the inside of the castle,
and surely shall find the heart of my Joan, and
if I keep my vow and neither eat nor drink here
or say aught but ask for that which I seek,
nothing can harm me."

So he sat down contentedly to wait for what
might come.   There he sat the whole night, and
no one came near him, but the birds sang so
beautifully that he almost forgot how the time
passed.

When morning dawned and light again
shone through the windows, he searched everywhere for some way out of the room, but the

door had quite disappeared. Moreover, the feast had gone from the table. The day passed, and still he was all alone, and as evening again drew in he sat and lamented, quite wearied out and faint for want of food. But when the darkness came, the lamps about the room were suddenly lit as if by magic, and all was brilliant, and a curtain was drawn aside, and there came in a little child with bright eyes and hair, who held in one hand a goblet and in the other a well-filled plate. These she placed before Michael, saying, " My mistress sends you these, and begs that you will eat and drink, for you must be both hungry and thirsty;" but Michael pushed away the goblet and the plate, and said,

" I seek the heart of Princess Joan ; I beg you to give it to me."

To this the seeming child answered nothing, but still pressed on him the food and wine. Then Michael took from his bosom the magic glass and looked through it, and saw no lovely child, but the same yellow hag with shrivelled face and evil eyes. With a cry of rage she dis-appeared, and though Michael searched everywhere, he could not find the way by which she went.

Now indeed he began to feel that unless he ate he could not live much longer, and wept from very weakness.

"Still I will neither eat nor drink," he said, "till I have found what I came to seek, and the fairy cannot refuse me much longer."

Night passed and day came, and he lay upon a couch quite still, too weak to move, yet he feared to sleep lest some spell should be thrown upon him.

So he lay all day, and as evening again drew near he began to feel despair, for he knew that in another day he would be dead of hunger.

"Oh! Why have I toiled for seven years," he cried aloud, "and at last won my way into the castle, if now I am to be starved to death, and Joan will never know how I have laboured for her sake?"

"And why should you be starved to death, my Prince?" said a voice; and at once the lights lit themselves, and into the room stepped the figure of the Princess Joan just as he had seen her last, dressed in white and gold, and in one hand bearing a golden goblet filled with clear ruby-coloured wine.

Michael gave a cry of joy and held out his arms to clasp her in them, but as he did so the sword sprang as it hung at his side, and he remembered his vow and drew back and gazed at her without speaking.

She knelt down beside him and raised the goblet to his lips, saying softly, " My poor love, how long you have worked for me ! Pray drink now, that you may be refreshed ere we two start for our home."

Then as he looked at her face and saw how beautiful she was his heart wavered, and he thought, " Can it be my Joan, and that I have truly won her ?" and almost had he let her place the wine at his lips, while with one hand she stroked his hair and murmured to him the while in a soft voice, when the cup struck against the magic glass in his bosom, and he drew it forth and looked at her, and he trembled with horror and disgust, for there he saw no lovely Princess

Joan, but the same yellow hag, who held in one skinny hand a goblet, formed from a skull, from which she would have him drink.

Michael sprang to his feet and dashed it from him, and the ruby wine poured on the floor, and there followed an awful noise like a peal of thunder, and the room was full of smoke, and wild cries were heard.

He grasped the sword and sat still, trembling all over ; but when the smoke cleared away the whole aspect of the room was changed; the silken hangings, and gold, and pearls, and flowers, were all gone, and he was sitting in a grim gray chamber like a vault, and in front of him stood the yellow hag, whose eyes shone spitefully and her lips laughed wickedly ; but in one hand she held what it made Michael rejoice to see.   It was a soft pink feathery thing, with wings, but shaped like a heart, and it trembled and quivered in her hand.

"Take it," she cried, "for well have you won it.   Take it, and tell the Queen how many years of toil and labour her proud words and boasting have cost.   Then when you see her, from whom it was stolen, let it fly, but first say over it these words :—

> " Heart of Joan
> Lost and won
> Fly back home,
> Thy journey's done.
> Take back joy
> Take back pain
> Heart of Joan,
> Fly home again."

and it will fly to her side, and you will see it no more ; and now begone."

Michael seized the heart with a cry of joy and exultation, and then turned and fled from the room through an open iron door, and passed through the passages, no longer softly carpeted and hung with silk, but dreary and bare, made of cold stone, down which his footsteps echoed and clashed.

He hurried from the castle as quickly as might be, and once outside did not stop to look for the old man or the monster, but swam the moat, and went straight to where his boat lay moored as he had left it, nearly seven years before, and never paused till he had rowed so far that the gray castle and the shore had almost passed from view. At last he came again to the shore where he had bought his boat of the fishermen, and here he went on land, and started to walk till he had reached Joan's country, and her father's castle.

He had no money, and his clothes were rags, his hair was thin and gray, and his shoulders bent. He looked like a poor beggar, and he had to beg food as he went, or he would have been starved. Still, he was ready to cry for joy, because he took with him the little soft heart he had gone so far to find.

He trudged on both day and night, making great haste, for he knew that the seven years were almost gone, and he was afraid lest already he might be too late, and find that Joan had married some one else. At last, after many weary miles, he reached her country, and drew near to the palace where she lived, and here he found that the people were all decorating their houses, and making preparations as if for some great festival.

He stopped and begged for food from a

woman who stood by a cottage door, and when she had given him some bread, as he ate it he asked her to tell him what went on in the country, and why there was such rejoicing.

"It is for the marriage of the King's daughter Joan," said the woman; "To-morrow she is to be married to old King Lambert, and the wedding will be very grand, but none of the country folk like it, for he is old and ugly, and they say he does not love her at all, but only marries her that he may be king of this country as well as his own. The Queen is in sore distress about it, and for seven years refused her consent; but they will be over to-morrow, and so they will be wed, and the guests are already beginning to arrive at the palace, and each one brings some splendid gift."

"I will be a guest at that wedding," cried Michael; "And I bring the best gift of all for the bride;" and he hurried on again, not heeding the woman's scorn and laughter.

When he came to the palace, he found that it was hung with flags, and arches of flowers were erected in front of it, and grand lords and ladies, and servants stood at the door to receive the guests who came.

Michael went as near as he dared, afraid lest he should be driven away by the servants, and then he saw a little foot-page, and he went to him and said,

"Please tell me where is the Princess Joan, and what she is doing."

"She is sitting with the King and Queen and King Lambert in the state-room, to receive the guests and accept the presents they bring," said the page.

"I am a guest, and I bring a present for her," cried Michael; "Tell me how I shall get into the palace that I may give it to her."

On hearing this the page burst out laughing, and told the other servants what he said. And they were very angry, and seized Michael, and some would have ducked him in the pond, and some would have taken him before the King, but they said, "Not now—wait till the wedding is over to-morrow, and then we will see how he

will punish the beggar-man for his imperti-
nence."

So they took him off to a stone tower outside the garden gates and thrust him into it,
and locked the door, and there was only one
little window high up and barred across with
bars, and from it he could see the palace and
the gardens.

Then at last he gave way to despair. "Of
what avail were all my years of toil, and for
what am I gray and old before my time," he
cried, " if after all, when I have earned that for
which I worked so long, I may not give it to
Joan, but must remain a prisoner and see her
pass by to marry some one else?" and he threw
himself on the ground and cried aloud.

At night as he lay and mourned, he heard
sounds of merrymaking, and music and laughter
from the castle. Sometimes he called out, "Joan !
Joan ! I am here—I who have worked for you
for years, and brought home your stolen heart,
and now will you wed King Lambert in spite of
all?" sometimes he beat against the bars of the
prison window, but all in vain, and at last, when

all sound had ceased from the castle, he lay silent upon the ground, caring no more for life.

When the sun rose, and there was again a stir without, he got up and looked from the window, and saw the old nurse who walked by herself in the garden, and she looked very sad. Then Michael called out, "Do you not know me? You at least, who bid me go, and praised me then, should remember me now." On hearing this the old nurse drew near the prison window, and looked at him, and said, "Who are you, and why are you here? My eyes are old, and my ears are deaf, but I think I have seen you, and heard your voice before."

"Seven years ago," said Michael, "I too was a bridegroom, who came to wed your Princess, and for seven long years have I worked, that I might bring home to her the heart she had not. Go and ask your Queen, why she has broken her pledge to wait for seven years, till Prince Michael should return."

"Prince Michael! Is it really Prince Michael?" cried the old nurse joyfully. "And

you come in time, for our Princess is not
married yet, and she must pass by here, on her
way to church.   So you shall call to her as she
passes by, and speak for yourself."

"Then keep near and tell me when she
comes," said Michael, "lest she go by without
seeing me."

Presently the whole castle was astir, and
trumpets were sounding, and clarions ringing.
Then when the sun was high, Michael heard the
tramping of horses, and the sound of music, and
the old nurse said to him, "Here she is," and
he looked between the bars of the prison window
and saw a grand procession, and his heart gave
a bound, for in their midst, in a golden gown,
and seated on a white palfrey, was Princess
Joan, and she looked just as lovely as when he
went away seven years before.

On one side of her rode her father and
mother, and the Queen's face was most mournful, and her eyes were red with crying.   On
the other rode an ugly old man, whom Michael
guessed to be King Lambert, and he smiled
and bowed to the people, but they muttered

and grumbled, when they looked at him, and
saw how ugly and wicked, he looked.

When Michael saw them coming, he took
from his bosom the little pink heart, and stroked
it fondly as he whispered over it,

> "Heart of Joan
> Lost and won
> Fly back home,
> Thy journey's done.
> Take back joy
> Take back pain
> Heart of Joan,
> Fly home again ;"

and at once it spread its wings and fluttered
through the bars of the prison, and over the
heads of the people, who shouted, "Look at
the pink bird!"   For a moment it rested at the
side of the Princess Joan, and then disappeared.
She gave a scream, and cried,

"My mother! My father! What has happened? Oh see, it is Michael who has returned!" and ere they could stop her she had
turned her palfrey's head towards the prison
window, and pushed her white arms through the
bars to clasp the Prince.

"—— and ere they could stop her she had turned her palfrey's head towards the prison window, and pushed her white arms through the bars to clasp the Prince."—P. 128.

"Michael, my love!" she cried, "How gray and worn you are now. How hard you must have laboured for me through these long years. Now, how shall I pay you, save by loving you all my life!" and she tried to beat down the bars of the prison window.

When the people heard her, they cried, "It is Prince Michael, who went seven years ago, and who we all thought was dead, and he is returned in time to marry our Princess. Now will we indeed have a wedding, and she shall marry the Prince who has toiled so long for her;" and King and Queen and people laughed for joy. 'Twas in vain for King Lambert to rage, and cry that the Princess was betrothed to him.

"Nay!" said the Queen, "She has been pledged to Prince Michael for seven years. We are grieved for your sake, King Lambert, but we cannot break our royal word."

Then the people burst into the prison and brought out Michael, all torn and gray as he was, and Princess Joan kissed him before them all, and begged that he would marry her at once, that every one might see how well she

K

loved him and how grateful she was. So they brought a fine white horse with a grand gold saddle, and jewelled bridle, and placed Michael upon it, and he rode to church beside the Princess, and married her, and the people threw flowers before them, and bells rang and trumpets sounded, and all were glad.

And when it was done Michael was dressed in purple and gold, and messengers were sent to his father and mother and the old wizard, that they might come and see how he had come home victorious, and rejoicings filled the whole country.

"For now we are sure of a good King," the people said. "See, he has already shown what he can do. Surely no one else could ever have found the heart of Princess Joan."

" Good-day, friend," said he.   " If you have nothing to do, perhaps you would not mind carrying my load for me for a little."—P. 131.

PEDLAR was toiling along a dusty road carrying his pack on his back, when he saw a donkey grazing by the way-side.

"Good-day, friend," said he. "If you have nothing to do, perhaps you would not mind carrying my load for me for a little."

"If I do so, what will you give me?" said the donkey.

"I will give you two pieces of gold," said the pedlar, but he did not speak the truth, for he knew he had no gold to give.

"Agreed," said the donkey. So they journeyed on together in a very friendly manner, the donkey carrying the pedlar's pack, and the pedlar walking by his side. After a time they met a raven, who was looking for worms in the roadside, and the donkey called out to him,

"Good-morrow, black friend. If you are going our way, you would do well to sit upon my back and drive away the flies, which worry me sadly."

"And what will you pay me to do this?" asked the raven.

"Money is no object to me," said the donkey, "so I will give you three pieces of gold." And he too knew he was making a false promise, for he had no gold at all to give.

"Agreed," said the raven. So they went on in high good humour, the donkey carrying the pedlar's wares, and the raven sitting on the donkey's back driving away the flies.

After a time they met a hedge-sparrow, and the raven called out to it,

"Good-day, little cousin. Do you want to earn a little money? If so, bring me some worms from the bank as we go along, for I had no breakfast, and am very hungry."

"What will you give me for it?" asked the hedge-sparrow.

"Let us say four pieces of gold," said the raven grandly; "for I have saved more during my long life than I know how to spend." But he knew this was not true, for he had not saved any gold at all.

"Very well," said the hedge-sparrow, and so on they went, the donkey carrying the pedlar's pack, and the raven keeping the flies away from the donkey, and the hedge-sparrow bringing worms to the raven.

Presently they saw in the distance a good-sized town, and the pedlar took out from his pack, some shawls and stuffs and hung them over the donkey's back that the passers-by might see, and buy if they were so disposed. On the top of the other goods lay a small scarlet blanket, and when he saw it the hedge-sparrow said to the pedlar,

"What will you take for that little blanket? It seems to be a good one. Name your price and you shall have it whatever it is, for I am badly in want of a blanket just now ;" but as the hedge-sparrow had not a penny in the world, he knew he could not pay for it.

"The price of the blanket is five pieces of gold," said the pedlar.

"That seems to me to be very dear," said the hedge-sparrow. "I don't mind giving you four pieces of gold for it, but five is too much."

"Agreed," said the pedlar, and he chuckled to himself and thought, "Now I shall be able to pay the donkey, otherwise I might have had some trouble in getting rid of him."

The hedge-sparrow flew to the raven's side and whispered in his ear, "Please to pay me the four pieces of gold you owe me, for we are coming to a town, and I must be turning back."

"Four pieces of gold is really too much for bringing a few worms," said the raven. "It is absurd to expect such payment, but I will give you three, and you shall have them almost immediately," and he bent down over the donkey's ear and whispered,

"My friend, it is time you paid me the three pieces of gold which you promised, for the pedlar will stop at this town, and you will not have to go farther with him."

"On thinking it over," said the donkey, "I have come to the conclusion that three pieces of gold are really a great deal too much to give for having a few flies driven away. You must have known that I was only joking when I said it, but I will let you have two, though I consider that it is much more than the job was worth;" and the donkey turned again to the pedlar, saying, "Now, good sir, your two pieces of gold, if you please."

"In a moment," said the pedlar, and turning to the hedge-sparrow, said, "I really must have the money for the blanket at once."

"So you shall," answered the hedge-sparrow, and cried angrily to the raven, "I want my money now, and cannot wait."

"In an instant," answered the raven, and again whispered to the donkey, "Why can't you pay me honestly? I should be ashamed of trying to slip out of my debts in such a way."

"I won't keep you waiting a second," said the donkey, and he turned once more to the pedlar and cried, "Come, give me my money. For shame! a man like you trying to cheat a poor beast like me."

Then the pedlar said to the hedge-sparrow, "Pay me for my blanket, or I'll wring your neck."

And the hedge-sparrow cried to the raven, "Give me my money or I'll peck out your eyes."

And the raven croaked to the donkey, "If you don't pay me, I'll bite off your tail."

And the donkey again cried to the pedlar, "You dishonest wretch, pay me my money or I'll kick you soundly."

And they made such an uproar outside the walls of the town, that the beadle came out to see what it was all about. Each turned to him and began to complain of the other loudly.

"You are a set of rogues and vagabonds," said the beadle, "and you shall all come before the mayor, and he'll settle your quarrels pretty quickly, and treat you as you deserve."

At this they all begged to be allowed to go away, each one saying he did not care about being paid at all. But the beadle would not listen to them, and led them straight away to the market-place, where the mayor sat judging the people.

"Now, whom have we here?" cried he. "A pedlar, a donkey, a raven, and a hedge-sparrow. A set of worthless vagabonds, I'll be bound! Let us hear what they have to say for themselves."

On this the pedlar began to complain of the hedge-sparrow, and the hedge-sparrow of the raven, and the raven of the donkey, and the donkey of the pedlar.

The mayor did not heed them much, but he eyed the pedlar's pack, and at length interrupted them, and said,

"I am convinced that you are a set of good-for-nothing fellows, and one is quite as bad as the other, so I order that the pedlar be locked up in the prison, that the donkey be soundly well thrashed, and that the raven and the hedge-sparrow both have their tail-feathers pulled out, and then be turned out of the town.

As for the blanket, it seems to me to be the only good thing in the whole matter, and as I cannot allow you to keep the cause of such a disturbance, I will take it for myself. Beadle, lead the prisoners away."

So the beadle did as he was told, and the pedlar was locked up for many days in the prison.

"It is very sad to think to what straits an honest man may be brought," he sighed to himself as he sat lamenting his hard fate. "In future this will be a warning to me to keep clear of hedge-sparrows. If the hedge-sparrow had paid me as he ought, I should not be here now."

Meantime the donkey was being soundly well thrashed, and after each blow he cried,

"Alas! alas! See what comes to an innocent quadruped for having to do with human beings. Had the pedlar given me the money he owed, I should not now be beaten thus. In future I will never make a bargain with men."

The raven and the hedge-sparrow hopped out of the town by different roads, and both were very sad, for they had lost all their tail feathers, which the beadle had pulled out.

"Alas!" croaked the raven, "my fate is indeed a hard one. But it serves me right for trusting a donkey who goes on his feet and cannot fly. It is truly a warning to me never again to trust anything without a beak."

The hedge-sparrow was quite crestfallen, and could scarcely keep from tears. "It all comes of my being so taken in by that raven," he sighed. "But I should have known that these large birds are never honest. In future I will be wise, and never make a bargain with anything bigger or stronger than myself."

THE BREAD of DISCONTENT

ONCE there was a baker who had a very bad, violent temper, and whenever a batch of bread was spoiled he flew into such a rage, that his wife and daughters dared not go near him. One day it happened that all his bread was burnt, and on this he stamped and raved with anger. He threw the loaves all about the floor, when one, burnt blacker than the rest, broke in half, and out of it crept a tiny thin black man, no thicker than an eel, with long arms and legs.

"What are you making all this fuss about, Master Baker?" said he. "If you will give me a home in your oven I will see to the baking of

" If you will give me a home in your oven I will see to the baking of your bread, and will answer for it that you shall never have so much as a loaf spoiled."—P. 141.

your bread, and will answer for it that you shall never have so much as a loaf spoiled."

"And pray what sort of bread would it be, if you were in the oven, and helped to bake it?" said the baker; "I think my customers might not like to eat it."

"On the contrary," said the imp, "they would like it exceedingly. It is true that it would make them rather unhappy, but that will not hurt you, as you need not eat it yourself."

"Why should it make them unhappy?" said the baker. "If it is good bread it won't do any one harm, and if it is bad they won't buy it."

"It will taste very good," replied the imp, "But it will make all who eat it discontented, and they will think themselves very unfortunate whether they are so or no; but this will not do you any harm, and I promise you that you shall sell as much as you wish."

"Agreed!" said the baker. So the little imp crept into the oven and curled himself into the darkness behind, and the baker saw no more of him.

But next day he made a great batch of bread, and though he took no heed of the time when he put it in, and drew it out, just as he wanted it, it was done quite right—neither too dark nor too light—and the baker was in high good humour.

The first person who tasted the bread was the chief justice. He came down to breakfast in high spirits, for he had just heard that an old aunt was dead, and had left him a great deal of money. So he kissed his wife and chucked his daughters under the chin, and told them that he had good news for them. His old aunt had left him twenty thousand pounds in her will. On this his wife clapped her hands for joy, and his daughters ran to him and kissed him, and begged him to let them have some of it. So they all sat down to breakfast in great glee, but no sooner had the justice tasted the bread than his face fell.

"This is excellent bread," he said, taking a large slice; "I wish everything else were as good;" and he heaved a deep sigh.

"Why?" cried his wife, who had not yet begun to eat. "This morning, I am sure, there is nothing for you to complain of."

" Nay !" said the mayor ; " it is very nice to
have twenty thousand pounds, but think how
much nicer it would have been if it had been
thirty.   How much more one could have done
with that ! Or even if it had been twenty-five
thousand pounds, or even twenty-one.   Twenty-
one thousand pounds is a very nice sum of money,
but twenty thousand pounds is no good at all.
I am not sure that it would not be better not to
have had any."

" Nonsense !" cried his wife, who was now
eating her breakfast also ; " you are very wicked
to be so discontented ; but one thing I do say.
It would have been much nicer if we had had it
when we were young and better able to enjoy
it.   Money is very little use to people at our
time of life.   It would have been really nice if
we had had it fifteen years ago.   As it is, I can't
say I care much for it, and it makes me sad to
think we did not get it before."

" Nay," cried the daughters ; " in that case
how much better it would have been for us to
have it instead of you ; we are young, and
able to enjoy ourselves, and we could have

given you a little of it if you'd liked, but we could have been very happy with the rest; as it is, it is no pleasure to us."

So they fell to quarrelling about the money, and by the time breakfast was done, they all had tears in their eyes, and felt discontented and unhappy.

The next person to eat the bread was the village doctor. All night long he had been sitting up with a man who had broken his leg, and he had feared lest he should die, but as morning came he saw he would live, so he returned home to his wife in very good spirits, although he was sadly tired. The wife had already had her breakfast, but she had made all ready for her husband, with a loaf of the baker's new bread.

"See, dear husband," she said, "here is your breakfast, and some nice bread quite new, because I know you like it. How glad we ought to be, that this poor man is likely to live."

"Yes, indeed," said the doctor; "being up all night is tiring work, but I don't grudge it when I know that it does some good," and then he began to eat. "I am not sure, after all, that I have done such a good thing in curing this man. It is true that his broken leg hurt him very much, but perhaps when he is well again, he may break his back, and that would be much worse. Perhaps I had better have left him to die. I daresay when he is quite well, all kinds of misfortunes will befall him; I had much better have let him alone."

"Why," cried his wife in surprise, "what are you saying, husband? Are you not a doctor, and is it not your business to cure people? And when you succeed ought you not to be glad?"

"I wish I were not a doctor," said the husband, sighing. "It would be much better if there were no doctors at all;" and he sat and lamented, and nothing his wife could say, could cheer him.

In a pretty little cottage near the doctor's house lived a young couple, who were newly married, and were as happy as the day was long. Their cottage was covered with roses, and filled with pretty things, and they had everything their hearts could desire. This morning they both came down smiling and happy, and the young wife kissed her husband, and sang for joy. So they sat down to breakfast, chattering like two birds in a nest; but no sooner had the husband tasted the bread than his face fell, and he was silent for a time; then he said,

"It is a very terrible thing to think how happy we are, for it cannot last. Something melancholy is sure to happen to us, and till it comes we shall live in dread of it; for we know happiness never lasts, and this is a thought that makes me very sad."

The wife had now also taken some bread.

"What is this you are saying?" she said. "How can you think such dreadful things? I do not like you when you talk like that; and I think it is very hard for me to be married to a man who wants to be unhappy."

"The best thing we can hope for," said the husband, sighing, "is for some great misfortune to befall us; then we should be all right, for we should know then, that we knew the worst that

could come.   As it is we shall live in suspense
all our days."

" Now," cried his wife, " I am indeed unfortunate.   What could be worse than to have
a husband who does not like being happy ?   I
wish I had married some one else; or indeed
had no husband at all."

So both began to grumble, and at last
to quarrel, and finally both were crying with
anger.

Not far out of the village was a large
pleasant farmhouse, standing amongst fields, and
the farmer was a hale, bright man, with a good
wife and pretty children.   He was very busy
just now getting in the corn, for it was autumn,
and he stood among his men, directing them as
they worked in the fields.   He had not had
time to have a proper breakfast before going
to work, but his wife sent some out to him
with some of the baker's new bread, and he
sat down under a tree to eat it   As he did
so he looked up at the farmhouse, and thought,
with pride, that it was the largest farm in all
the country round, and that it had belonged to

his father, and his grandfather, and his great-grandfather, before him.

"'Tis a fine old house, for sure," thought he, as he took a large piece of bread, "'Tis so well built and strong;" but no sooner had he swallowed a mouthful than his thoughts changed.

"What should I do if it were to fall down and crush me some day," he said to himself. "After all, 'tis only built of brick, and might tumble any day. How much stronger it would have been if it had been built of stone. Then it would not have been nearly so likely to give way. Really when my great-grandfather built it he should have thought of this. How selfish all men are;" and he became quite unhappy lest his house should fall, and lamented while he ate.

In the kitchen the farmer's wife was very busy cooking and cleaning, and scarcely stopped to eat till near mid-day. Then she took up a piece of bread and cheese, and leant against the window as she ate it, that she might watch for her eldest girl and boy, Janey and Jimmy, who would now be returning from school.

"Our baker really bakes very decent bread," said she; "'tis almost as good as my own;" and she went on eating till she saw her two children coming through the fields together.

"Here they come," said she; "How bonny they look. Really I ought to be very proud of them. I don't know which is the prettier, Janey or Jimmy, but 'tis a pity, for sure, that Janey is the eldest. It would be much better if Jimmy were older than she. 'Tis a bad thing for the sister to be older than the brother. Now, if he were her age, and she were his, that would be really nice, for then he could take care of her and see after her; but, as it is, she will try to direct him, and boys never like to obey their sisters; I really almost think I had better not have had any children at all," and the tears filled her eyes, and when her girl and boy ran in to her, her face was very sad, and she seemed to be scarcely glad to see them.

So things went on all over the village. Each one as he tasted the bread grew discontented and angry, till at last all the people went about grumbling and complaining, or else shedding tears outright. Only the baker himself was cheerful and merry, and sang as he kneaded his dough, and sold it to his customers with a light heart, for his trade had never been so good. Every atom of bread he made was sold at once, so he cared not one whit for the trouble of the other people, and laughed to himself when he heard them complaining, and thought of the words of the dark little elf.

One day as he stood kneading at the door and whistling to himself, the doctor walked past and looked angrily at him.

"What on earth are you making that whistling for?" he asked. "I declare one would think that you were as happy as a man could be."

"And so I am," said the baker, "And so I should think were you too, for you have nothing to trouble you."

"Nothing to trouble me, forsooth!" cried the doctor in a rage. "How dare you insult me in this way? I tell you what it is, my fine fellow, I think you are very impertinent, and if I have any more of your impudence I will take my stick and thrash you soundly. It really is not to be borne, that one man should be allowed to tell another that he has nothing to complain of."

" Nay, *you* can have as much to complain of as you like, so long as I have not," cried the baker, and he laughed loudly. This only made the doctor angrier still, and he was just going to seize the baker when up came the farmer.

" Was there ever such a village as this ? " he cried. " It is not fit for any one to live in, there is always such fighting and quarrelling going on. What is the matter here ? "

" Matter enough," cried the doctor. " Here is a fellow dares to tell me I have nothing to complain of, nor he either."

" This is monstrous ! " said the farmer ; " he deserves to be hung. How dares he say such a thing on such a wretched day as this, with such a blue sky and such a bright sun ? "

" Why, Master Farmer," cried the baker, " yesterday you grumbled because it was raining, and now you grumble because it is fine."

"And I tell you that it is enough to make one grumble," said the farmer. "It should have been fair yesterday, and should have rained to-day. You ought to be ashamed of such talk, Master Baker, and I think it would serve you justly right if we took you before the Justice and let us see what he thinks of your conduct."

"Nay!" cried the baker, beginning to be frightened, "what have I done that I am to be taken before the Justice?"

"What have you done, indeed!" said the doctor. "We will see if the Justice cannot find that out pretty quickly." So they seized the baker and dragged him away in spite of himself, and as they pulled him through the village the people thronged about them, and followed till there was quite a large crowd.

The Justice sat at his door smoking a pipe, with tears in his eyes.

"Now what is all this uproar for?" cried he. "Am I never to be left in peace? How hard is the life of a Justice!" but he got up and came out on the steps to meet them.

"See here," cried the doctor; "here is a man who says he has nothing to complain of, and we have brought him to you, to know if he is to be punished, or to be allowed to go on talking like this."

"Certainly not," cried the Justice, "or we shall soon have the whole village in an uproar. Let him be taken to the market-place, and I will order that he be publicly flogged by the soldiers."

At this the poor baker burst out crying, and entreated to be let off, saying that now indeed he had plenty to complain of, but at this the justice was angrier still. "Then," said he, "you certainly deserve to be flogged for having told an untruth before, when you said you had not. Take him away, and do as I bid."

So they dragged the baker off to the market-place, and made a ring round him, so that he could not escape, and then there came down two or three soldiers with ropes in their hands, and they seized him, and began to beat him before all the crowd.

But by this time all the people were so en-
raged against him, that a number of them cried,
"Let us go to his house and pull it down." So
off they ran to the baker's house, and broke the
windows and knocked about the furniture, and
then some of them fell on the oven, and
wrenched off the door, and others seized the
pokers and tongs, and smashed in its sides, and
in the hurry and scuffle, the little dark man
crept out of the oven and scuttled away unseen
by any one. But no sooner had he gone than
a great change came across the people.

The soldiers on the green stopped beating
the baker, and looked at each other aghast, and
the Justice called out,

"Stop! What is all this uproar about?
And what has this man done that you are
beating him without my orders?" and the
people in the crowd whispered to each other;
"It is true,—what has he done?" and they
slunk away, looking ashamed.

The Justice also at first looked somewhat
ashamed of himself, but he drew himself up,
and looking very important, said,

"There, my man, you are forgiven for this once, and now go your way, and see that you behave better in future;" and then he walked away with much dignity.

So the baker was left alone in the market-place, and he cried for rage and pain.

"This all comes of the oven imp," cried he, as he limped home. "Directly I get home I will drive him out of my oven, and away from my house. Better to have a hundred batches of bread spoiled than to be flogged for saying one is happy." But when he reached his house the little dark man was nowhere to be found; there was nought but the broken oven with its sides battered in.

The baker mended the oven, and from that time forth his bread was just like other people's; but for all that he had learnt to be quite contented, for now he knew that there were worse things than having his loaves burnt black, and he was only too well pleased to take his chance with other people, without the help of fairy folk. As for the little black imp, he was never heard of more, and the people in the village soon recovered their good humour, and were just as happy and contented as they had been before they tasted the bread of discontent.

LD King Roland lay upon his
death-bed, and as he had no
son to reign after him he
sent for his three nephews,
Aldovrand, Aldebert, and
Alderete, and addressed them
as follows :—

"My dear nephews, I feel that my days are
now drawing to an end, and one of you will
have to be King when I am dead. But there
is no pleasure in being King. My people have
been difficult to govern and never content with
what I did for them, so that my life has been a
hard one, and though I have watched you all
closely, still I know not, which is most fit to
wear the crown ; so my wish is that you should

each try it in turn. You, Aldovrand, as you are the oldest, shall be King first, and if you reign happily, all well and good; but if you fail, let Aldebert take your place; and if he fail, let him give it up to Alderete, and then you will know which is the best fitted to govern."

On this the three young men all thanked their uncle, and each one declared that he would do his best, and soon after old King Roland died and was buried with great state and ceremony.

So now Aldovrand was to be King, and he was crowned, and there were great rejoicings everywhere.

"'Tis a fine thing to be King," cried he in much glee; "Now I can amuse myself and do just as I please, and there will be no one to stop me, and I will lie in bed as late as I like in the morning, for who dares blame one, if one is King?"

Next morning the Prime Minister and the Chancellor came to the palace to see the new King and settle affairs of state, but they were told that his majesty was in bed and had given orders that no one should disturb him.

"This is a bad beginning," sighed the Prime Minister.

"Very bad," echoed the Chancellor.

When they came back to the palace later in the day the King was playing at battledore and shuttlecock with some of his gentlemen, and was very angry at being interrupted in his game.

"A pretty thing," he cried, "That I the King am to be sent for hither and thither as if I were a lacquey. They must go away and come another time;" and on hearing this the Prime Minister and Chancellor looked graver still.

But next morning there came the Commander-in-Chief and the Lord High Admiral, as well as the Prime Minister and the Chancellor, all wanting to have an audience with the King, and as he was not out of bed and they could not wait any longer, they all stood outside his bedroom door, and knocked to gain admittance, and at last he came out in a towering rage, and throwing them his crown, cried,

"Here, let one of my cousins be King, for I will not bear this longer. It is much more trouble than it is worth, so Aldebert or Alderete may try it and see how they like it, but as for me, I have had enough of it," and he ran downstairs and out of the palace door, leaving the Prime Minister and the Chancellor and the General and Admiral staring at each other in dismay.

Aldovrand walked out of the town unnoticed, and turned towards the country, whistling cheerily to himself. When he had gone some way in the fields, he came to a farmhouse, and in a meadow near, the farmer stood talking to his men. Aldovrand went straight up to him, and, touching his hat, asked if he could give him any work.

"Work?" cried the farmer, little thinking he was talking to his late king. "Why, what sort of work can you do?"

"Well," said Aldovrand, "I am not very fond of running about, but if you want any one to mind your sheep, or keep the birds from your corn, I could do that nicely."

"I tell you what you can do if you like," said the farmer. "I am wanting a goose-boy to take care of my geese. See, there they are on the common. All you will have to do is to see that they don't stray away, and to drive them in at night."

"That will suit me exactly," cried Aldovrand. "I will begin at once;" and he went straight on to the common, and when he had collected the geese together lay down to watch them in high good humour.

"This is capital," he cried, "and much better than being King at the palace. Here there is no Prime Minister or Chancellor to come worrying;" and he lay watching the geese all day very contentedly.

When the Prime Minister and the Chancellor knew that Aldovrand was really gone, they went in a great hurry to Aldebert to tell him that it was his turn to be King. But when he heard how his cousin had run away, he looked frightened.

"I will do my best," quoth he; "but I really know very little about the matter. However, you must tell me, and I will do whatever you direct."

M

At hearing this the Prime Minister and the Chancellor were delighted.

"Now we have got the right sort of King," they said; and both wagged their heads with joy.

So King Aldebert was crowned, and there were great rejoicings all over the country.

Early next morning he was up all ready to receive his Ministers, and first came the Prime Minister.

"Your Majesty," said he, "I come to you on an affair of much importance. A great part of our city is falling down, and it is very necessary that we should rebuild it at once. If you will command it, therefore, I will see that it is done."

"I have no doubt you are right," said the King; "pray let them begin building at once;" and the Prime Minister went away delighted.

Scarcely had he gone when in came the Commander-in-Chief.

"Your Majesty," said he, "I wish to lay before you the state of our army. Our soldiers have had a great deal of fighting to do lately, and are beginning to be discontented, but the late King, your uncle, would never attend to their wants."

" Pray do what you like," said King Alde-bert.

" To satisfy them," said the Commander-in-Chief, " I think that we should double their pay. This would keep them in a good humour, and all will go well."

" By all means, that will certainly be the best way," said Aldebert. Let it be given to them at once ;" and on hearing this, the Commander-in-Chief went away right merrily.

When he had gone, there came in the Chancellor with a long face.

" Your Majesty," he said, " I have this morning been to the treasury, and I find that there is scarcely any money left. The late King, your uncle, spent so much in spite of all I could say, that now it is almost all gone. Your Majesty must now save all you can for the next year or two, and you ought also to lower the soldiers' pay, and stop all public works."

" I have no doubt you are quite right," cried

the King. "You know best, let it be done as you wish."

But next morning in came the Prime Minister with a frowning face. "How is this, your Majesty?" cried he. "Just as we are beginning our buildings, the Chancellor comes and tells us that we are not to have any money to build with." He had not done speaking when the Commander-in-Chief burst into the room unable to conceal his rage.

"Yesterday your Majesty told me that all the soldiers should have double pay, and this morning I hear, that instead of that, their wages are to be lowered!" Here he was interrupted by the Chancellor, who came running in looking much excited,

"Your Majesty," he cried, "did you not yesterday say we were now to begin saving, and that I was not to allow any more money to be spent, and that the army must do with less pay?"

And then all three began to quarrel among themselves. When he saw how angry they were, King Aldebert took off his crown and said,

"I am sure you are each of you quite right; but I think I am scarcely fit to be a King. Indeed I think you had better find my cousin Alderete, and let him be crowned, and I will seek my fortune elsewhere." And he had slipped out of the room, and run downstairs and out of the palace, before they could stop him.

He went briskly down the highroad into the country, the same way that Aldovrand had gone.

After he had gone some way, he met a travelling tinker who sat by the roadside mending tin cans, with his little fire at his side.

Aldebert stood watching him, and at last said, "How cleverly you mend those holes! You must lead a pleasant life, going from house to house in the green lanes mending wares. Do you think I could learn how to do it if you would teach me?"

The tinker, who was an old man, looked at him and said,

"Well, I don't mind giving you a trial if you like to come with me, for I want a strong young man sometimes to help me wheel my little cart, and I'll teach you my trade, and we'll see what you can make of it."

So Aldebert was delighted, and went with the tinker.

When they knew he was really gone the Prime Minister and the Chancellor looked at each other in dismay.

"This will never do," cried they; "we must go at once to Prince Alderete; and let us hope he may do better than his cousins."

When Prince Alderete heard that it was his turn to reign he jumped for joy.

"Now," cried he, "at last I will show what a king should really be like. My cousins were neither of them any good, but they shall now see how different I will be."

So he was crowned, and again there were great rejoicings all over the country.

Next day he sat in state to receive the Chancellor and Prime Minister and hear what they had to say.

"My friends," said he to them, "a good King ought to be like a father to his people, and this is what I mean to be. I mean to arrange everything for them myself, and if they will only obey me, and do as I direct, they are sure to be both prosperous and happy."

On hearing this both Prime Minister and Chancellor looked anxious, and the Chancellor said,

"I fear, your Majesty, your people will not like to be too much meddled with." At this the King was very angry, and bid them see about their own business, and not presume to teach him his.

When they had gone he went to take a drive in his city, that he might see it and know it well; but directly he returned to the palace he sent for the Prime Minister, and when he had arrived, said,

"I already see much to be altered in my kingdom. I do not like the houses in which many of the people dwell, nor indeed the dresses they wear ; but what strikes me most of all is, that wherever I go I smell a strong smell of pea soup. Now, nothing is so unwholesome as pea soup, and therefore it would not be right

in me to allow the people to go on eating it.   I
command, therefore, that no one shall again
make, or eat pea soup, within my realm on pain
of death."

Again the Prime Minister looked very
grave, and began to say,

" Your Majesty, your subjects will surely not
like to be hindered from eating and drinking what
pleases them !"   But the King cried out in a rage,

" Go at once and do as I bid you."   So the
Prime Minister had to obey.

Early next morning when the King arose
he heard a great hubbub under his window, and
when he went to see what it was, he saw a vast
mob of people all shouting, " The King, the
King !   Where is this King who would dictate
to us what we shall eat and drink ?"

When   he   saw   them   he   was   terribly
frightened, and at once sent off for the Prime
Minister and Chancellor to come to his aid.

" Pray go and tell them to eat what they
like," he cried when they arrived ; " But, do you
know, I find it will not at àll suit me to be
King.   You had best try Aldovrand, or Alde-

bert, again;" and, so saying, he took off his crown and laid it down, and slipped away out of the palace before either Prime Minister or Chancellor could stop him.

He went out of the back door, and ran, and ran, and ran, till he had left the town far behind, and came to the country fields and lanes—the same way that his two cousins had gone; and as he went he met a sweep trudging along carrying his long brooms over his shoulder.

"My friend," cried Alderete, stopping him, "Of all things in the world I should like to be a sweep and learn how to sweep chimneys. May I go with you, and will you teach me your trade?"

The sweep looked surprised, but said, "Yes, Alderete could go with him if he chose, and as he was now going on to the farmhouses, on the road, to sweep the chimneys, he could begin at once." So Alderete went with the sweep, carrying some of his brooms for him.

After a time the people outside the palace grew quiet, when they heard that the King would not interfere with them further. And when all was again still, the Prime Minister and Chancellor went to seek the King, but he was nowhere to be found in the palace.

"This will never do," cried they. "We must have a King somehow, so we had best have back one of the others." So they started to look for Aldovrand or Aldebert.

They sought them all over the city, and at last they came into the same country road down which the three cousins had gone, and there they saw Aldovrand lying in a meadow watching his flock of geese.

"Good day, my friends," cried he when he saw them; "And how are things going on at the palace? I hope my cousins like reigning better than I did. Now, here I lie peacefully all day long and watch my geese, and it is much nicer than being King."

Then the Prime Minister and Chancellor told him all that had happened, and begged that he would come back with them to the palace again, but at this Aldovrand laughed outright.

"Now, here I lie peacefully all day long and watch my geese, and it is much nicer than being King." —P. 170.

"No indeed!" cried he, "I would not be
King again for any man living. You had
best go and seek my cousin Aldebert, and ask
him. I saw him go down the road with a
tinker, helping him to mend his tins. So go
and ask him, and leave me to mind my geese
in peace."

So the Prime Minister, and the Chancellor
had to seek still farther.

They trudged on and on, till at last
they met Aldebert, who sat by the side of
the road mending a tin kettle, and whistling
cheerily.

"Heyday, whom have we here?" cried he.
"The Prime Minister and the Chancellor! And
I am right glad to see you both. See how
clever I have grown; I am learning to be a
tinker, and I mended that hole all myself."

Then the Prime Minister and Chancellor
begged him to leave his pots, and come back
to the palace and be King, but he fell to work
again, harder than ever, and said,

"No indeed; go and ask my cousins, who
are both much cleverer than I. I really don't

do for it at all, but I make a very good tinker, and I like that much better."

"Then what can we do?" cried the Prime Minister, "for we don't know where Alderete has gone."

"I saw him go by here with a sweep a little time ago," said Aldebert; "and he went into that farmhouse yonder, so you had best seek him there."

So the Prime Minister and the Chancellor went on to the farmhouse. At the door stood the farmer's wife, but when they asked her if she had seen the King go by, she stared with surprise.

"Nay," said she; "no one has been here but our sweep and his apprentice. He is in there sweeping the chimney now." On hearing this, the Prime Minister and Chancellor at once ran into the farmhouse, and saw the old sweep standing by the kitchen fireplace. "And where is the other sweep?" cried they. "He is gone up the chimney, and is just going to begin sweeping," said the old man. "So if you want to speak to him you must shout." So they shouted and called,

"King Alderete, King Alderete!" as loud as ever they could, but he did not hear. Then the Chancellor knelt in front of the grate, and put his head up the chimney, and called,

"King Alderete, King Alderete! It is the Prime Minister and I, the Chancellor, come to fetch your Majesty back to the palace."

When Alderete heard him up the chimney, he trembled in every limb, but he replied,

"I'm not going to come down; I don't want to be King. I am going to be a sweep, and I like that much better. I shan't come down till you are gone away, and now you had best go quickly, for I am going to begin sweeping, and all the soot will fall on your head," and then they heard the rattle of the broom in the chimney, and a whole shower of soot fell on the Chancellor's head.

The Prime Minister and the Chancellor turned back to the city very disconsolately. "We must go and look for a King elsewhere," they said. "It is no use troubling about

Aldovrand, Aldebert, and Alderete." So they left the one to his geese, and one to his tins, and the other to sweep chimneys, and that was the end of the three clever Kings.

NCE upon a time lived a King whose wife was dead and who had one little daughter who was named Fernanda. She was very good and pretty, but when she was a child she vexed all her ladies by asking them questions about everything she saw.

"Your Highness should not wish to know too much," they told her, whereat Princess Fernanda threw up her little head, and said,

"I want to know everything."

As she grew up she had masters and mistresses to teach her, and learnt every language and every science; but still she said, "It is not enough; I want to know more."

In a deep cave underground there lived
an old Wizard who was so wise that his face
was well-nigh black with wrinkles, and his long
white beard flowed to his feet.   He knew all
sorts of magic, and every day and night sat
poring over his books till now there seemed to
be nothing left for him to learn.

One night after every one was asleep, Princess Fernanda rose and slipped softly down the
stairs and out of the palace unheard by any
one, and stole away to the Wizard's cave.

The old man was sitting on his low stool
reading out of an immense book by a dim green
light, but he raised his eyes as the ·Princess
entered at the low doorway, and looked at her.
She wore a blue and silver robe, but her bright
hair was unbound, and fell in ripples to her
waist.

"Who are you, and what do you want with
me?" he asked shortly.

"I am the Princess Fernanda," she said,
"and I wish to be your pupil.   Teach me all
you know."

"Why do you wish for that?" said the

Wizard : "you will not be better or happier for it."

"I am not happy now," said the Princess sighing wearily. "Teach me and you shall find me an apt pupil, and I will pay you with gold."

"I will not have your gold," said the Wizard, "but come to me every night at this hour, and in three years you shall know all I do."

So every night the Princess went down to the Wizard's cave while all the court were sleeping. And the people wondered at her more and more, and said, "How much she knows! How wise she is !"

When the three years had gone by the Wizard said to her, "Go! I can teach you no more now. You are as wise as I." Then the Princess thanked him and went back to her father's palace.

She was very wise. She knew the languages of all animals. The fishes came from the deep at her call, and the birds from the trees. She could tell when the winds would rise, and when the sea would be still. She could have turned her enemies to stone, or

N

given untold wealth to her friends. But for all that, when she smiled, her lips were very sad, and her eyes were always full of care. She said she was weary, and her father thought she was sick, and would have sent for the physicians, but she stopped him.

" How should physicians help me, my father," she said, "seeing that I know more than they ?"

One night, a year after she had taken her last lesson from the Wizard, she arose and returned to his cave, and he raised his eyes and saw her standing before him as formerly.

"What do you want ?" he said. " I have taught you all I know."

"You have taught me much," she said, falling on her knees beside him, "yet I am ignorant of one thing — teach me that also — *how to be happy*."

" Nay," said the Wizard with a very mournful smile ; " I cannot teach you that, for I do not know it myself. Go and ask it of them who know and are wiser than I."

Then the Princess left the cave and

" Then the Princess left the cave and wandered down to the sea-shore."—P. 178.

wandered down to the sea-shore. All that night she spent sitting on a rock that jutted out into the sea, watching the wild sky and the moon coming and going behind the clouds. The sea dashed up around her, and the wind blew, but she did not fear them, and when the sun rose the waters were still and the wind fell. A sky-lark rose from the fields and flew straight up to heaven, singing as though his heart would burst with pure joy.

"Surely that bird is happy," said the Princess to herself; and she called it in its own tongue.

"Why do you sing?" she asked.

"I sing because I am so happy," answered the lark.

"And why are you so happy?" asked the Princess.

"So happy?" said the lark. "God is so good. The sky is so blue, and the fields are so green. Is that not enough to make me happy?"

"Teach me, then, that I may be happy too," said Princess Fernanda.

"I cannot," said the lark; "I don't know how to teach;" and then he rose, singing, into

the blue overhead, and Princess Fernanda
sighed and turned back towards the palace.

Outside her door she met her little lap-dog,
who barked and jumped for joy on seeing her.

"Little dog," she said; "poor little dog, are
you so glad to see me? Why are you so
happy?"

"Why am I so happy?" said the little dog,
surprised. "I have plenty to eat, and a soft
cushion to rest upon, and you to caress me. Is
not it enough to make me happy?"

"It is not enough for me," said the Princess,
sighing; but the little dog only wagged his tail
and licked her hand.

Inside her room was the Princess's favourite
little maid Doris, folding up her dresses.

"Doris," she said, "you look very merry.
Why are you so happy?"

"Please your Royal Highness, I am going
to the fair," answered Doris, "and Luke is to
meet me there; only," she added, pouting a little,
"I wish I had a pretty new hat to wear with
my new dress."

"Then you are not perfectly happy, so you

cannot teach me," said Princess Fernanda, and then she sighed again.

In the evening at sunset she arose, and went out into the village, and at the door of the first cottage to which she came, sat a woman nursing a baby, and hushing it to sleep. The baby was fat and rosy, and the mother looked down at it proudly.

The Princess stopped, and spoke to her.

"You have a fine little child there," she said. "Surely you must be very happy."

The woman smiled.

"Yes," she said, "so I am; only just now my goodman is out fishing, and as he's rather late, it makes me anxious."

"Then you could not teach me," said the Princess, sighing to herself as she moved away. She wandered on till she came to a church, which she entered. All was still within, for the church was empty; but before the altar, on a splendid bier, lay the body of a young man, who had been killed in the war. He was dressed in his gay uniform, and his breast was covered with medals, and his sword lay beside

him.   He was shot through the heart, but his
face was peaceful and his lips were smiling.
The Princess walked to his side, and looked at
the quiet face.   Then she stooped and kissed
the cold forehead, and envied the soldier.   " If
he could speak," she said, "he surely could
teach me.   No living mouth could ever smile
like that."   Then she looked up and saw a
white angel standing on the other side of the
bier, and she knew it was Death.

"You have taught him," she said, holding
out her arms.   "Will you not teach me to
smile like that?"

"Nay," said Death, pointing to the medals
on the dead man's breast, " I taught him whilst
he was doing his duty.   I cannot teach you."
And so saying he vanished from her sight.

She went out from the church down to the
sea-shore.   There was a high sea, and a great
wind, a little child had been playing on a row
of rocks, and had slipped off them into the
water, and was struggling among the waves,
and would soon be drowned, for he was beyond
his depth in the water.

When the Princess saw him, she plunged into the water and swam to where the child was, and taking him in her arms, placed him safely on the rocks again, but the waves were so strong that she could scarcely keep above them. As she tried to seize the rocks, she saw Death coming over the water towards her, and she turned to meet him gladly.

"Now," said he, clasping her in his arms, "I will teach you all you want to know;" and he drew her under the water, and she died.

* * * * *

The King's servants found her lying on the shore, with her face white and her lips cold, but smiling as they had never smiled before, and her face was very calm. They carried her home, and she was laid out in great state, covered with gold and silver.

"She was so wise," sobbed her little maid, as she placed flowers in the cold hand, "she knew everything."

"Not everything," said the skylark from the window; "for she asked me, ignorant though I am, to teach her how to be happy."

"That was the one thing I could not teach. her," said the old Wizard, looking at the dead Princess's face. "Yet I think now she must be wiser than I, and have learned that too. For see how she smiles."

www.ingramcontent.com/pod-product-compliance
Lightning Source LLC
Chambersburg PA
CBHW020612030726
47497CB00007B/2209